About Shoma Narayanan

Shoma started reading Mills & Boon® romances at the age of eleven, borrowing them from neighbours and hiding them inside textbooks so that her parents didn't find out. At that time the thought of writing one herself never entered her head—she was convinced she wanted to be a teacher when she grew up. When she was a little older she decided to become an engineer instead, and took a degree in electronics and telecommunications. Then she thought a career in management was probably a better bet, and went off to do an MBA. That was a decision she never regretted, because she met the man of her dreams in the first year of business school—fifteen years later they're married with two adorable kids, whom they're raising with the same careful attention to detail that they gave their second-year project on organisational behaviour.

A couple of years ago Shoma took up writing as a hobby (after successively trying her hand at baking, sewing, knitting, crochet and patchwork), and was amazed at how much she enjoyed it. Now she works grimly at her banking job through the week, and tries to balance writing with household chores during weekends. Her family has been unfailingly supportive of her latest hobby, and are also secretly very, very relieved that they don't have to eat, wear or display the results!

TM

Take One Arranged Marriage...

Shoma Narayanan

MILLS & BOON

First published in Great Britain 2013
by Mills & Boon, an imprint of Harlequin (UK) Limited.
Harlequin (UK) Limited, Eton House, 18-24 Paradise Road,
Richmond, Surrey TW9 1SR

© Shoma Narayanan 2013

ISBN: 978 0 263 23405 3

Harlequin (UK) policy is to use papers that are natural, renewable and recyclable products and made from wood grown in sustainable forests. The logging and manufacturing process conform to the legal environmental regulations of the country of origin.

Printed and bound in Great Britain
by CPI Antony Rowe, Chippenham, Wiltshire

Also by Shoma Narayanan

Monsoon Wedding Fever

**Did you know these are also available as eBooks?
Visit www.millsandboon.co.uk**

TM

To Badri, Aditya and Anousha for putting up with me
on the days I spent every free minute writing—
you guys are the best family ever!

PROLOGUE

The Times of India—*matrimonial section:*

*'Very successful lawyer, good-looking, 33, height
6 ft 2 inches, South Indian, Bengaluru-based,
seeks beautiful high-caste Hindu, well-educated,
as bride.'*

TARA looked up in disbelief.

'You guys answered this? Without checking with me
first?' Her temper was rising swiftly and her mother
gave her a wary look.

'Your father thought…' she began.

'I didn't know he could think,' Tara said, whisking the
newspaper cutting from her mother's hand. One length-
wise tear, fold, tear again. There. One successful lawyer, ready for the dustbin. She carried the pieces across
and threw them in. 'If they write back, tell them I'm not
interested,' she said.

'It's not so simple, Tara,' her mother said. 'They're
coming over this evening—the parents are at least.'

Tara stared.

'That was…fast,' she said. 'Wasn't that yesterday's

newspaper? Are these people really desperate? Or are you that keen to get rid of me?'

'No, we're not,' her mother protested, looking unhappy.

Tara relented, putting an arm around her and steering her to a chair. 'Tell me all about it,' she said. 'Till yesterday I thought you guys wanted me to become a schoolteacher and give up my "stupid plans" to do a PhD in a strange city.' Her face darkened as she remembered the recent fight with her father. 'Now you want me to marry a good-looking lawyer. Six feet, two inches, no less. What's going on?'

'He's Mr Krishnan's son,' Tara's mother explained. 'Mr Krishnan's the new general manager at the plant, and he happened to mention he'd put out this ad...'

Tara let a low whistle out through her teeth. Now, *that* explained a lot. Her dad was a lowly supervisor at the steel manufacturing plant—his daughter marrying the GM's son would be the ultimate in social enhancement, something like marrying into royalty. This needed some thinking through. Bengaluru... Tara's brain was racing. It could work. As long as she figured out how to manage it smartly. Marriage at twenty-two was *not* what she'd planned. But it beat running away from home— something she'd been seriously considering over the past few days.

'We wouldn't force you into anything,' her mother was saying, her worn face looking even more anxious than usual.

'We' meant her father, of course. The last thing Tara's mother had forced her into was a pair of pink dungarees when Tara was three. Tara had hated pink, and the dungarees hadn't lasted five hours. But her father was a different story. His parental style was very closely aligned to the 'because-I'm-your-father-and-I-said-so' school of thought, and he and Tara had clashed since the day Tara learnt to talk. Her mother had been stuck in the middle for the last twenty years, too scared to contradict her husband even if she secretly sympathised with Tara.

'It's a very good family,' her mother continued, looking at her daughter appealingly. 'I know you wanted to study further, but we might not get an opportunity like this again. It's not as though you have anyone else in mind. And the son is really good-looking.'

Tara frowned. Her mother's definition of good-looking was deeply suspect—it was likely that the man looked like a Bollywood movie star from the eighties, complete with shaggy hair and oversized tinted spectacles.

'He is,' her mother insisted, holding out a photo. 'Take a look.'

Tara dutifully took a look, and then a second one. For once her mother wasn't wrong: the man was gorgeous. Either that or the photographer was really good with an airbrush. She leaned closer, and her mother held on to the photo convulsively, obviously scared it might share the fate of the newspaper cutting.

'Relax, I won't do anything to it,' Tara said impatiently. The man was definitely hot, all rugged features and sexy smile, but she'd reserve judgement till she actually met him. Maybe he'd have a stammer, or a dreadful accent, or be totally unappealing neck downwards—it *was* a head shot—or have BO.

'When is His Highness the General Manager coming over?' Tara asked.

Her mother looked at her in alarm. 'Don't talk like that!' She grabbed Tara's hand. 'He's your father's boss's boss—we can't afford to offend him. Keep your tongue under control while they're here, Tara, please. If only for my sake. If you don't want to marry his son you don't have to. I'll speak to your father.'

Tara could appreciate the truly heroic effort her mother was making to promise something like that, and her heart melted. She leaned across and hugged her. 'You won't have to. I'll speak to him myself if I need to. Don't worry—I won't let you down.'

She never had. When it came to choosing between getting her own way against her father and keeping her mother relatively happy she was a push-over. Her mother won hands-down every time. That was the main reason she hadn't left home yet—though there had been practical considerations as well. Her father held the purse strings, and she'd thought it would be difficult to manage on her own, at least at the beginning. That bit was now sorted, with a friend having promised to lend her some money, but she was still hesitant.

One of the drawbacks of being brought up in a stereotypical traditional Indian family was that you ended up unconsciously buying into a lot of traditional Indian values. Bringing shame to the family was something your soul kicked against even when your brain was telling you that you were being an idiot.

Running away would *definitely* bring shame to the family. No one in the small industrial town they lived in would believe that a man was not involved. Her father would find it difficult to keep his head up in society, her mother's friends would make condescending remarks, and all in all, their life would be a living nightmare. And in spite of all her father's blustering and bullying, his archaic parenting style, Tara loved him a lot. The love was buried very, very deep down, but it was there—she couldn't help it—and she knew he loved her back. His heart would be broken if he knew his daughter had run away because she couldn't bear living in the same house as him any longer. She couldn't do that to him unless it was absolutely necessary.

'What's the guy's name?' she asked. 'The general manager's son?'

'Vikram,' her mother said, happy that Tara was finally taking an interest. 'It's an unusual name for a South Indian, but his parents have lived in Mumbai ever since they got married, so they must have decided on a North Indian name.'

Tara nodded, as her mother twittered on. Vikram... Hmm... Gorgeous, sexy and successful Bengaluru-based Vikram Krishnan didn't know it, but he just might be the answer to all her problems.

CHAPTER ONE

TARA looked at the photograph she'd saved on her phone, and then up again at the passengers alighting from the air-conditioned section of the train. There were several families whom she ignored, her eyes searching for a man travelling alone. That one, maybe? No, he looked too old—forty at least, or even older. And the next man getting off alone was almost completely bald.

Maybe Vikram Krishnan wasn't on this train after all, she thought, her heart sinking. Maybe his flight into Kolkata had got delayed, and he'd missed the connecting train to Jamshedpur. She punched a small fist into the palm of her other hand in an unconscious gesture, and more than a few people on the busy platform turned to look at her curiously.

So far her plan had seemed to have a reasonable chance of success. The general manager and his wife had turned out to be an extremely likeable couple—for a few minutes Tara had actually caught herself wishing her parents were more like them. She'd set out to charm them and had succeeded, having them laughing at her carefully self-censored little jokes and practically eating out of her hand in a few minutes. They'd told her parents eagerly that they thought she'd be 'perfect' for Vikram.

Now Vikram was coming down to Jamshedpur for the express purpose of meeting her and deciding whether she was worthy of becoming his wife—Tara involuntarily curled her lip at the thought—and all she needed to do was to catch him alone before he came to her house to inspect her. Her parents had said that he'd told them not to meet him at the station, but it seemed the ideal opportunity. Assuming she could find him, that was.

There was a flurry near the door of the compartment opposite her as an elderly lady carrying two suitcases and a Peke got jammed in the doorway. A porter tried to extricate her as the Peke yapped wildly and a bunch of excited relatives on the platform shouted encouragement. Tara's attention was drawn to them for a few seconds and she almost missed seeing a tall, well-built figure push open the other door of the compartment, and swing lightly down onto the platform.

It was definitely the man in the photograph—though he looked a little older, and harder somehow. Tara pulled up the image once again to make doubly sure. It was blurred, a shot of the original that she'd clicked sneakily on her phone's camera when her mother wasn't paying attention. Same man. No doubt about it.

Vikram Krishnan had taken his luggage down and was now surveying the crowded station with deep-set jet-black eyes, his slanting eyebrows giving him a rather cynical look. In spite of the cold his jacket was slung over one shoulder. He was wearing designer jeans and a long-sleeved white shirt open at the collar, and he looked like a model for something foreign-sounding and expensive. As Tara watched, he waved away the red-coated porters milling around him and, picking up his suitcase with one capable-looking hand, started walking towards the exit.

Now that she'd finally spotted him, Tara felt a large part of her confidence desert her. He looked so *big,* for one, and so terribly sure of himself. She'd been crazy to think he'd even want to listen to her.

His long strides had taken him halfway down the platform before she managed to gather her wits and run after him. The platform was full of people, and Tara found herself falling behind. 'Sir!' she called out, and then 'Mr Krishnan! Vikram!' He didn't seem to hear her, though several other people turned to stare. 'Vikram! Sir!' she yelled again, hurrying after him.

He stopped finally. Tara was gasping a little by the time she caught up with him, and she felt the last bits of her courage ooze out of her as she looked up at his forbidding expression.

'You want to speak to me?' he asked.

His voice was deep, with a gravelly undertone that was so unexpectedly sexy it took her completely off guard. When she kept on staring at him without answering, he raised an eyebrow and repeated the question in Hindi.

'I'm Tara,' she said, and then, when he looked at her uncomprehendingly, she made a helpless little gesture. 'I met your parents a few days ago. My dad works with yours...' He still looked blank, and Tara abandoned the roundabout approach. 'They're looking for a wife for you, right? They want you to meet me—you're supposed to come over to our house tomorrow.'

If she'd been looking for a lightbulb moment it wasn't forthcoming. 'There's only one girl they've asked me to meet,' he said. 'And her name's Naina, or something like that.'

'Naintara,' she said. 'Most people call me Tara.'

'Right,' he said, frowning. 'I'm sorry, I'm a little confused. Why are you here if we're supposed to meet tomorrow?'

'It's…complicated.' Tara said. 'Can we sit down somewhere? I won't take long.' Her heart was pounding in her chest, and all her well-rehearsed speeches had flown out of her head. She was not normally susceptible to even the most good-looking men, and her reaction to Vikram had thrown her off balance.

Vikram led the way to the station canteen, pulling out one of the plastic chairs for her before sitting down himself. 'Coffee or tea?' he asked.

Tara said, 'Coffee.'

He turned to give the waiter their order, and Tara waited till the waiter had gone before she spoke again.

'I need to ask you a couple of things,' she said. 'Are you really serious about this whole arranged marriage thing? Or are you here just to humour your parents?'

Vikram didn't look annoyed by the questions, but he did think a little before he answered.

'I'm serious about an arranged marriage,' he said finally. 'But I'm not planning to blindly marry someone my parents choose, if that's what you mean.'

'Right,' Tara said. 'And do you have plans to move out of Bengaluru any time soon? Like in the next three or four years?'

This time he looked puzzled, his forehead creasing a little. 'No,' he said. 'I'm pretty much permanently settled there.'

There was a brief silence. Tara had run out of questions and was wondering how to embark on an explanation of her behaviour. 'I know this must seem odd, my turning up to meet you like this,' she said, giving Vikram her most winning smile.

'It's unusual, I admit,' he said, smiling back.

Tara was struck again by quite how good-looking he was. He looked like a completely different person when he smiled, his eyes losing their rather grim expression and the corners of his firm mouth tilting up boyishly.

'Maybe you could tell me a little more about why you're here?' he said. 'I assume there is a point to your questions?'

'Oh, yes,' Tara said. 'It's this—I've got a place in the Institute of Science at Bengaluru to do my doctorate in environmental studies and my dad is refusing to let me go. He thinks I've studied enough, and he's desperate to get me married off. I told him I'm not interested, and he said he wouldn't force me, but he won't let me go to Bengaluru, either. The maximum he's willing to do is allow me to become a schoolteacher till he manages to palm me off onto someone.' She paused a little, a troubled look on her vibrant face. 'I could ignore him and go, of course, but now my mum's told me that they've spoken to your parents, and you're from Bengaluru...'

Her voice trailed off, and Vikram continued the sentence for her. 'And marrying me would please your parents *and* get you to Bengaluru? Is that it?'

She nodded, her big eyes absurdly hopeful as she stared at him across her coffee cup. 'It did seem like the ideal solution,' she admitted. 'Assuming we hit it off, of course.'

Vikram leaned back in his chair, surveying her silently. She'd turned out to be a surprise in more ways than one, and he was at a stage in life when very few people surprised him. She was very direct, and very clear about what she wanted—both traits that he'd come to think of as uncommon in women. And her looks... His mother had told him that she was pretty, but 'pretty' didn't begin to cover the allure of frank, intelligent eyes set in a heart-shaped face, and the mischievous smile trembling on her lush red lips. She wasn't very tall, but the proportions of her slim body were perfect. And her hair was lovely—thick, straight and waist-length. A jolt of lust took him by surprise, turning his academic appreciation of her looks into something more urgent and immediate.

'Why is doing your doctorate so important?' he asked, partly to break the silence and partly because he genuinely wanted to know. 'And especially one in environmental science? Aren't the career options rather limited?'

Tara flushed a little. People kept asking her that, and she tended to get a bit worked up and annoyed about it. 'I've always wanted to be an environmentalist,' she said, in what she hoped was a calm and neutral-sounding voice. 'I'd be getting an opportunity to work with one of the most well-known scientists in the field, and the research facilities at the institute are world-class. As for career options—I want to lead my own research team one day. Science isn't a very well-paying field, but I'll earn enough to get by.'

'If you marry me you won't have to worry about money,' Vikram pointed out.

Tara gave him an appalled look. The money angle of

marrying him hadn't struck her at all, and for a second she'd been so busy defending her choice of career that she'd forgotten the reason she was talking to him. Now he probably thought she was out for a cushy corporate wife lifestyle while she played at being a scientist.

'If you don't marry me I'll have to worry about it,' she said, recovering quickly. 'My stipend won't be enough to keep a cat alive. I'll need to work part-time until I complete my doctorate. But I think it's worth it.' The last bit came out sounding a little defiant, because Vikram's expression was unreadable and she couldn't help feeling that she wasn't convincing him.

She was wrong, though—Vikram was intrigued. He didn't come across too many starry-eyed idealists in his line of work, and Tara's unshakeable confidence in her dream was impressive and oddly endearing at the same time.

'Worth it?' he asked, stretching the words out a little. 'Even worth marrying someone you hardly know as long as you get to complete your degree?'

'That part's a little complicated,' Tara muttered, hoping he wouldn't ask her anything more right then. She didn't want to explain the situation with her parents until absolutely necessary.

Thankfully, he didn't probe further, instead asking abruptly, 'How old are you anyway?'

'Twenty-two,' Tara said, and as a nasty thought struck her she bubbled into further speech. 'I hope you're not thinking of talking to my dad about this? He'll burst a blood vessel if he finds out I came here to meet you. If you decide not to marry me tell your parents you don't like the shape of my nose or something. Or say I'm too short. I'll figure some other way out.'

'But you'll go and enrol for that PhD, no matter what?' Vikram said. 'Relax, I'm not planning to tell him.' His lips twitched slightly. 'And, for the record, I quite like the shape of your nose.'

'Really?' she asked. Distracted from her immediate woes, she put up a hand to touch it. 'Everyone says it ruins my face—too snub.'

'Snub is cute,' Vikram said, standing up and touching her hair gently, sending an unexpected thrill through her body. 'I need some time to think, and it's time I left. We're meeting tomorrow in any case—you can call me on this number if you need to talk.'

'OK,' Tara said, taking the card with his mobile number.

She managed to flash a smile at him as he said goodbye in the car park, but she felt deeply despondent. He'd sounded more like an indulgent older brother than someone even remotely interested in marrying her.

The next day Vikram sat silently in Tara's parents' living room, listening to his parents making polite conversation with her father. Tara's father had so far not made a very good impression. He was over-eager to please, and his wife—an older, washed-out version of Tara—was obviously scared of him. Tara herself had not made an appearance yet, and Vikram was getting impatient.

He cut into a long-winded description of Tara's various accomplishments and said pointedly, 'Maybe she could tell us more herself?'

'Of course, of course,' Mr Sundaram said effusively.

'You must be eager to meet her.' He turned to his wife and said in an angry undertone, 'Get Tara here quick. She should have been ready hours ago.'

'I thought you said...' his wife began, and then quailed under her husband's glare.

'I'll call her right away,' she said hurriedly, and left the room.

She came back with Tara a few minutes later.

Vikram blinked. Tara was almost unrecognisable. The day before she'd been dressed in jeans and a loose sweater, with her long hair gathered back in a ponytail. Today she was wearing a pale-pink *salwar-kameez,* and her hair was done up in an elaborate braid. Huge dangly earrings swamped her tiny shell-like ears and she was wearing a *bindi* in the centre of her forehead. His initial impression was a picture of modest womanhood— except for her eyes, which had a little glint in them that hinted at her being less than pleased with the situation she found herself in.

'This is my daughter,' Mr Sundaram was saying proudly. 'Very well-educated, MSc in Botany, gold medallist. Tara, you've already met Mr and Mrs Krishnan.'

'Namaskaram,' Tara said, folding her hands in the traditional gesture.

Both the Krishnans beamed back, clearly enchanted by her. Vikram could see why—Tara looked the epitome of good daughter-in-law material, and in addition she was vibrant, intelligent and very pretty.

'This is their son, Vikram,' Mr Sundaram continued. 'Very successful lawyer.'

'Thirty-three years old, six feet two inches,' Tara said demurely. 'Bengaluru-based.'

Her father glared at her, but Vikram's parents burst out laughing.

'I told you the ad was a dumb idea,' Mr Krishnan said to his wife. 'Vikram's annoyed we put it in without telling him, and Tara thinks it's a joke.'

'Of course not, sir. How can you say such a thing?' Tara's father said immediately.

Vikram remembered that his father was Mr Sundaram's boss. That went a long way towards explaining his overly eager-to-please attitude.

'You can ask Tara what you want,' he was saying now, the ingratiating smile still in place. 'She's been very keen to meet you.'

The thought of conducting a stilted conversation under the eyes of both sets of parents obviously appealed to Tara as little as it did to him, because she shot him a quick look.

'I'd actually prefer to talk to her alone,' Vikram said crisply, and before anyone could suggest that they move to another room—or, worse, go outside and talk in the garden—he continued, 'I was thinking of taking her out for dinner tonight.'

Going by the stunned silence that greeted this, he might have been suggesting that he take her out and rape her in the bushes. Tara's father was the first person to find his voice.

He said weakly, 'But, son, we've made dinner. I mean Tara's made dinner. I thought it would be a good idea for you to sample her cooking...'

'I chop vegetables really well,' Tara said before she could stop herself.

She knew she was going to get into trouble with her

father later on, but *really!* Sample her cooking, indeed. Not that she couldn't cook, but for this occasion her mother had done everything—other than chop the vegetables. The whole charade was beginning to irritate Tara intensely—right from the fake smile her father had plastered on his face to the ridiculous earrings she'd been forced to wear.

'I'll leave my mother to judge her cooking,' Vikram said, as if Tara hadn't spoken. 'I'll take the car, Dad, I'll pick you up from here when I drop Tara off after dinner. OK by you, Tara?'

'Can I change first?' she asked. This time her mother gave her an appealing look, so Tara muttered, 'Oh, all right. I look like a Christmas tree in this, that's all.'

'Have a good time!' Vikram's mother called after them as they left the room together.

Tara's room was at the front of the house, and she stopped to pick up her handbag and a sweater before running outside. Vikram was holding the car door open for her, and she slid in with a muttered thank-you.

'Where do you want to go?' Vikram asked as he drove out of the lane.

'Mmph,' Tara said in response, her face obscured by the grey cashmere sweater she was trying to tug down over her head.

Vikram pulled to the side of the road, and waited patiently as she struggled. 'Do you need help?' he asked politely after a few minutes passed, and his prospective fiancée continued to wrestle with the sweater.

'Darn thing's caught on my earring,' Tara panted, lifting a corner of the sweater to reveal her flushed face.

'I should have taken the earrings off first. They're like bloody chandeliers.'

'Stop wriggling,' Vikram said, clicking the car light on and reaching across to disentangle the earring. Tara obligingly leaned closer, and he was treated to a sudden glimpse of cleavage. Despite himself Vikram found himself looking—he had to tear his eyes away and concentrate on getting the earring out of the delicate wool. 'Done,' he said finally, his voice coming out a little thicker than normal.

In addition to the cleavage, there had been soft skin at the nape of her neck that he hadn't been able to avoid touching several times. And she was wearing a perfume that managed to be sweetly innocent and madly tantalising at the same time—a lot like Tara herself, Vikram thought, before he shook himself. He'd been celibate too long, he thought cynically, if he was starting to get excited about touching a woman's ear.

'Thanks,' Tara said, giving him a cheeky little smile. 'I thought I'd be stuck inside that thing for ever, blundering around like a headless horseman.'

'You're welcome,' he said, his voice sounding a little cold even to his own ears. 'Now, where would you like to go for dinner?'

'I don't know,' Tara said cheerfully as she tugged off the annoying earrings and deposited them in her handbag. 'Dad always takes us to his club, but the food's horrible and all the waiters have known me since I was ten years old.'

'There's a restaurant in the new five-star hotel, isn't there?' Vikram asked, mentioning the only decent hotel he'd seen in the city. 'I don't know Jamshedpur very well. This is my first visit since my father got transferred here.'

Tara was busy scrubbing the lipstick off her lips with a tissue. 'I've never been there,' she said. 'It's too expensive for the likes of us.' A little too late she realised that the remark could be interpreted in several ways, and tried to correct herself. 'I mean Dad doesn't like eating out much. He says it's a waste of money. And when we *do* go out…'

'You go to his club.' Vikram said. 'You told me. How do I get to the hotel from here?'

'You take the next left and go straight for around five kilometres,' Tara said, sounding a little subdued.

Vikram glanced at her. She had managed to get her hair out of the complicated-looking braid it had been in and was now finger-combing it into obedience. It was really lovely hair, he thought, as she bent her head to dig in her purse for a scrunchie, and it fell over the side of her face like a jet-black curtain. An auto-rickshaw honked indignantly, and he turned his eyes hastily back to the road.

'What's the news on your PhD?' he asked.

'I spoke to my supervisor again,' Tara replied. 'She said she's willing to wait for me till January, but after that she's going to take on the next research applicant on her list.'

Vikram nodded, and she didn't dare to ask him if he'd made up his mind. Presumably, as he was taking her out to dinner, he hadn't decided definitely *not* to marry her. Or maybe he had, and he just wanted to tell her in person rather than on the phone. This was all very confusing, Tara thought, wrinkling up her nose and peeking quickly at his rather stern profile.

'You look quite different now,' Vikram remarked as Tara got out of the car at the hotel.

'Different from yesterday, or different from five minutes ago?' Tara asked.

'Both, actually,' Vikram said. 'Though I meant your in-car makeover. An immense improvement, if you don't mind my saying so.'

It was. Unlike the sweater she'd worn to the station, the plain grey one she was wearing now was clingy, outlining her slim curves perfectly. After several unsuccessful attempts at tying up her hair she'd let it hang loose—that and the kohl that she'd wisely not tried to rub off made her look older and way more sophisticated than she had earlier. Though a lot of the effect was neutralised by the way she now stared at the water feature in the foyer of the hotel. Vikram had the distinct feeling that if it weren't for his hand under her elbow, steering her towards the restaurant, she would run up to it and stick her hands under the shimmering cascade of water.

'This place is cool,' she said, her eyes sparkling as she slid gracefully into a chair opposite Vikram.

He nodded, oddly touched at her excitement. He'd been to scores of restaurants, with scores of women, but none of them had been so genuinely pleased with so little. She went through the wine list carefully, but shook her head when he asked her what she'd like to drink.

'Just a Coke please,' she said. 'I don't drink. I was just looking at the names of the wines.'

Even the waiter smiled indulgently as he wrote her order down. Vikram had been about to order a Chilean wine that he was rather fond of, but he changed his mind and ordered a mocktail instead.

'I'll get straight to the point,' he said after the waiter left. 'Are you really serious about marrying me to get to Bengaluru and do your PhD?'

She nodded. 'I'm sorry about yesterday,' she said awkwardly. 'You must have thought I was crazy, accosting you like that. But your parents happened to mention that you didn't want them meeting your train, and I thought that was the only opportunity I'd get to speak to you alone.'

'I'm glad you came,' he said. 'It just took me a little while to understand what you wanted. Your father's still absolutely against your studying further, is he?'

Tara nodded. 'You saw him today,' she said. 'Getting me married off to a good South Indian man is currently topmost on his priority list. If he isn't able to manage that, he's OK with me taking up a teaching job while he continues with the manhunt.' She looked straight into his eyes. 'Look, I don't want to put you on the spot,' she said. 'If you don't want to marry me that's perfectly OK. I understand.'

Vikram glanced away for a second. His motives for wanting to get married were complex, but his requirements were extremely simple. Pretty much any nice-looking, reasonably well-educated girl would do—Tara fitted the description, and he genuinely liked her.

'I think marriage will work for us if we're both clear about what the other person wants,' he said finally. 'I'm the first one to admit that I'm going about this in a rather cold-blooded way. At your age you probably expect romance and candlelit dinners and a fairytale wedding.'

Tara smiled, her face taking on an uncommonly wise expression. 'People have been getting married in India for centuries without even meeting each other before the ceremony. I guess we're lucky we've been born into a generation that has some choice. Or at least you do—I don't think my dad has quite realised which century he's living in.' She took in the look on Vikram's face and grinned. 'The short answer is no, I'm not looking for romance. Though I wouldn't mind a candlelit dinner now and then.'

'You haven't considered leaving home and striking out on your own?' Vikram asked. He found it a little difficult to believe that a girl as confident as Tara was so closely controlled by her father. Her body language when her father was around didn't suggest that she found him intimidating in the least.

'Oh, I have,' Tara said. 'Until you appeared on the scene it seemed to be my only option. But my dad would have cut me off from the family completely—and though he's a pain I wouldn't like that to happen. My mum would be lost without me.'

The last bit was believable, Vikram thought. Her mother was definitely under her father's thumb, and he could imagine Mr Sundaram making her life miserable if Tara left home against his wishes.

The waiter came up with their drinks, and Tara's eyes lit up as she saw the mocktail. 'Ooh, that looks cute,' she said, pointing at the little umbrella perched on top of the bright blue drink.

Vikram winced. 'You can have it if you want,' he said. 'I'm quite happy with a Coke.'

Tara exchanged the drinks and sipped at the blue mocktail. 'It's good,' she pronounced. 'It looks a bit like window-cleaning fluid, but it tastes nice.' She plucked the umbrella off the drink and tried opening and shutting it a few times, before looking up. 'You can ask questions now,' she prompted politely.

Vikram gave her a puzzled look. 'What questions?'

'Marriage interview questions,' she said. 'Aren't you supposed to quiz me on my hobbies, whether I can cook, how many children I'd like to have—that kind of thing?'

He laughed, and Tara found herself laughing with him.

'OK, here goes,' he said, entering into the spirit of the thing. 'We'll begin with a rapidfire round. What's your favourite book?'

'*To Kill a Mockingbird.* Yours?'

Vikram shook his head, his eyes dancing. 'No, I get to ask the questions. Movie?'

'*Three Idiots.* Except the bit where the guitarist guy hangs himself.'

'Music?'

'Classical Karnatic.' He looked surprised, and she laughed. 'My parents spent a bomb on lessons. It's kind of expected. Though, to be honest, it's grown on me.'

'Right. Food?'

'*Rasam* and rice.'

'Hmm, very traditional. Hobbies?'

'Science, trekking and crochet.'

'*Crochet?*'

He sounded incredulous, and Tara's ears went a little pink. 'Yes,' she said, trying to sound as firm as she could.

'Like Miss Marple? Fluffy wool and a little hooked needle?'

'Yes,' Tara said, her ears going pinker. But she stuck to her guns. 'It's creative and it's easy to carry around. Don't laugh.'

'I'm not,' Vikram said, looking so serious that Tara almost burst into giggles herself. 'I have immense respect for crochet. And trekking. But—if I may ask—crocheting what? And trekking where?'

'Crocheting purses for my mum and aunts, mainly.' Tara said. 'And trekking in the hills around the city—we had a group in college.'

'OK,' he said, consideringly. 'Now, what else. Pet hates?'

'Frogs. The city's overrun with them in the monsoons. I hate the way they look at me, as if they're expecting me to kiss them.' She gazed solemnly at Vikram, and his mouth twitched.

'Right,' he said. 'I hope I don't remind you of one?'

She put her head to one side. 'No. Though you're still a few kisses short of turning into Prince Charming.'

He raised his eyebrows, and Tara wondered if she'd gone too far. Talking of kisses had automatically drawn her eyes to his firm, uncompromising and perfectly shaped mouth, making her wonder what kissing him would be like. Quickly she looked away and continued, 'I mean, you're good-looking, but you're all dark and brooding—like something in a Gothic romance. Except when you laugh.'

'Thank you,' Vikram said politely. 'I don't think anyone's referred to me as Gothic before, but if that's the impression I've given I'll live with it.'

Tara flushed. She'd allowed her tongue to run away with her again, but what she'd said was true. When Vikram wasn't actively making an effort to be pleasant there was something remote and rather forbidding about him. And his height and undeniably impressive looks contributed to the effect.

She began to fiddle with the cocktail umbrella that was still lying on the table and he reached out, his fingers briefly twining with hers as he rescued it.

'Stop mangling the poor thing,' he said, putting the umbrella aside.

Tara stayed silent. The feel of his strong, lean fingers on hers had set up a little chorus of longing inside her, and she didn't know how to react.

'So, I'm done with my questions,' he said. 'Anything I've missed out?'

'You haven't asked me if I can cook,' she pointed out. 'My mother would be heartbroken. She's spent hours teaching me.'

'Ah, how could I have forgotten? So, have the lessons worked?'

'I think so,' she said cautiously. 'At least my father doesn't complain about my cooking any longer, and he's the fussiest eater on the planet.'

'I'm not fussy at all,' Vikram assured her. 'Besides, I employ a cook, so culinary skills aren't high on my list of suitable wifely qualities. Is there anything you'd like to ask?'

'Yes,' Tara said. 'There's something I really want to know. What made you agree to an arranged marriage in the first place? You don't seem the type.'

Vikram shrugged, his light-hearted mood dissipating a little. She was right—five years ago, if someone had told him he'd be marrying a woman his parents had chosen for him, he'd have laughed them out of the room. Things had changed a lot since then.

'Appearances can be deceptive,' he said lightly. 'I got tired of living alone, my parents would have found it difficult to adjust to a daughter-in-law from a different community—an arranged marriage just made more sense.'

It was a simplified version of the truth, and it would have to do till he got to know Tara better. He was still in two minds about marrying her. She was very attractive, but she was also very young—he felt positively ancient compared to her. A 'desi' Humbert Humbert with a legal-age Lolita. The thing that tilted the balance in her favour was the fact that she seemed absolutely transparent and straightforward. His last girlfriend had been a complex mass of half-truths and evasions, and he'd had enough of that to last a lifetime.

'Were you seeing someone?' Tara asked, her curiosity piqued by his reference to a daughter-in-law from another community.

Vikram, unused to answering questions about his personal life, was tempted to retort that it was none of her business. Then, as he met Tara's clear gaze, he realised that it *was* her business. She had just as much right to ask questions as he had—probably more, given that hers was a more vulnerable situation.

'I was dating a girl called Anjali for a while,' he said curtly. 'It didn't ever reach the marriage stage—she wasn't what I'd expect my wife to be.'

'What *do* you expect from your wife, then?' Tara asked in a low voice. The dismissive tone in which he'd spoken of Anjali jarred on her—he'd sounded uncaring, and just a little hard.

Vikram shrugged. 'I have a fairly busy social calendar because of my work. My wife would need to accompany me to parties and events, host people at our home. The house needs some work as well—I have a housekeeper and a cook, and they're both fairly efficient, but there's a lot that can be improved.' He smiled briefly, before continuing, 'Nothing much else that I can think of—except the obvious. Although I'm not keen on kids for a while, and I assume you aren't, either.'

Tara felt her cheeks heat up in spite herself. Kids. She'd never even thought of kids. She *had* thought of 'the obvious'—thought about it more often and for longer than she cared to admit. She'd even had an embarrassingly erotic dream about Vikram, which she'd been trying to push to the back of her mind. She stayed silent as he continued.

'I'm not a very demanding person. If we marry, you'd be free to lead your life the way you want. I travel a lot, and I work long hours. I won't be around much—I'd expect you to be independent and able to take of yourself.'

'That won't be a problem,' Tara said before she could stop herself. 'I'm not exactly the clingy type.'

'I know,' Vikram said, his lips quirking. 'From what I've seen of you so far, you seem to be about as clingy as The-Cat-That-Walked-by-Himself.'

Tara tried to frown, but ended up laughing. The discomfort she'd felt at the way he'd spoken about Anjali was gone—after all, she didn't know the full story. Perhaps Anjali had been one of those dreadful 'girlfriends from hell' kind of women? And Vikram looked so sexy when he smiled, she thought, it was impossible to think ill of him.

The food arrived, and Vikram skilfully guided the conversation towards Tara's plans to become an envi-

ronmentalist and specialise in the conservation of in-
digenous ecosystems. He didn't speak much, except to
interject with a question here and there. It was a ploy he
used often at work—making someone talk of something
they were passionate about to get them to reveal more
about themselves.

By the end of the meal he knew enough about the
ecosystems in eastern India to write a monograph on
the subject—he also knew a lot more about Tara than he
had before. His initial impression of her being extremely
intelligent was confirmed, and he'd developed a healthy
respect for her commitment to her research work.

'I'm sorry I talked so much,' she said as they walked
towards the car. 'I get a bit carried away when I'm talking about something that interests me.'

'You apologise way too often,' Vikram replied. He
took her hand gently as they stopped by the car. 'Tara,
I'd like to spend more time with you, to get to know you
better, but I know your parents won't be in favour of that.'

Here comes the brush-off, Tara thought despairingly,
while a separate part of her brain thrilled to the touch of
his hand. She'd handled this all wrong, she thought. She
should have let him do more of the talking. And ordering him to ask her questions had been a terrible move—
what could she have been thinking? And the worst thing,
quite apart from not being able to do her PhD if he didn't
marry her, was that in addition to thinking he was hot
she'd actually started liking him.

'So, given that it'll be difficult to get any more time
together, I guess we'll have to decide now.' Vikram took
a deep breath. 'Tara Sundaram, will you marry me?'

It came out sounding a lot cheesier than he'd intended, but the impact on Tara was satisfying. She looked stunned, staring at him with her pretty lips parted slightly, her breath coming a little faster. He realised he wanted to kiss her very badly, and to avoid succumbing to the temptation he released her hand, stepping back to lean against the car.

Tara took a few seconds to find her voice. 'Are you sure?' she asked finally, her voice sounding childish and more than a little shaky to her own ears.

Vikram nodded. 'I am. You'd be free to do your doctorate, work at whatever you want…' He raised a hand to tuck a lock of hair behind her ear, his hand lightly caressing her cheek.

For a second Tara had actually forgotten completely about her career aspirations, she was too busy trying to get her head around the fact that Vikram really wanted to marry her. When he mentioned the PhD, though, a rush of relief coursed through her.

'Thanks,' she blurted out.

Vikram winced. He wasn't sure what he wanted from her at this stage, but it definitely wasn't gratitude.

'Let's get back and tell our families, then,' he said, opening the door for her before walking around to slide into the driver's seat. 'I'm sure they'll be thrilled.'

Tara nodded silently, acutely aware of the awkwardness that had crept into the conversation. He was right— their parents would be thrilled. The magnitude of the step she was taking was just dawning on her, though, and an entire flock of butterflies seemed to have set up house in her stomach.

She clenched her hands together, willing herself to stay calm as they sped through the streets towards her parents' home. It was done now, she told herself firmly, sneaking a quick glance at Vikram's impassive profile. No turning back, even if she wanted to.

CHAPTER TWO

'WHERE would you two like to go for your honeymoon?'
Vikram's mother asked brightly. 'Europe?'

She and Vikram were at Tara's home to finalise some
of the arrangements for the wedding before Vikram went
back to Bengaluru. There were apparently a whole bunch
of auspicious wedding dates in November, just a little
over a month away.

Tara gulped. A honeymoon. That made the whole
thing sound a lot more real. She glanced at Vikram
quickly—as usual, it was difficult to gauge his reaction. Quite possibly he was as appalled at the thought of
a honeymoon as she was.

'I don't have a passport,' she said, trying to buy some
time.

It was perfectly true, anyway. She'd asked her father
once if she could get one and he'd sneered at the idea.
Serve him right, she thought nastily. He'd have one less
thing to brag about if she ended up going to Goa on her
honeymoon. He was at his insufferable best right now,
puffed up with pleasure at the thought of marrying his
daughter into the general manager's family.

Vikram's mother looked disappointed. 'Oh, dear. And
there isn't enough time to get one now. You might as well

get it done with your new surname after you're married. It'll have to be some place in India, then.' She got to her feet. 'I'll leave the two of you alone to discuss it.'

'Do you *want* to change your surname after we marry?' Vikram asked after his mother had left.

Tara gave him a startled look—it hadn't occurred to her that she had a choice in the matter. 'Isn't it expected that I change it to yours?'

'Who's doing the expecting?' he asked, raising his eyebrows. 'Not me, definitely, and I don't think anyone else's opinion counts.'

It probably didn't to him, but Tara herself didn't have the courage to be quite so careless of other people's views. Perhaps she'd get that way once she got away from her parents, she thought, her spirits lifting at the idea.

'Honeymoon destinations,' he said, as if the little interlude hadn't happened at all. 'Goa—Kerala—Rajasthan? Or something a little more out of the way?'

'I don't know,' Tara said flatly. 'I haven't been to any of them, so it's all the same to me.'

His face took on the remote expression that she'd mentally termed his switched-off face.

'No preferences at all? Beaches? Backwaters? Palaces? No dream holiday destination?'

She shrugged. 'Nowhere that's suitable for a honeymoon,' she said. 'I've always wanted to go on a tiger safari. We went to Gir for a vacation when I was kid, and saw lions in the wild, but I've only seen a tiger once, and that was in a zoo.'

'Let's do that, then,' Vikram said, surprising her. 'We can go to the Jim Corbett National Park, or to one of the reserves in MP—Bandhavgarh or Pench.'

'Won't that look a little odd?' Tara asked.

Characteristically, Vikram shrugged. 'It's our business where we go,' he said. 'I'll have to pull a few strings to get us a booking in time. And we can do Khajuraho either before or after.'

Tara's face promptly flamed in embarrassment—Khajuraho was famous for its erotic temple sculptures, and she did *not* want to spend the rest of her life having her leg pulled by people who knew she'd gone there on her honeymoon.

'OK, the Taj Mahal, then,' Vikram said, noticing her confusion. 'I suggested Khajuraho because it's in the same state as Pench, but if the idea bothers you we can go and see the Taj.' She looked unconvinced, and he added 'By moonlight?' in encouraging tones.

'I can't decide which would be worse,' she muttered, and he laughed outright.

Tara had decided quite early on that Vikram's laugh was one of the sexiest things about him, and an automatic little thrill ran through her. His laugh or his voice—the jury was still out on which was sexier. Maybe she should invite her friends to meet him and then do a poll. She realised suddenly that he was saying something, and gave him an enquiring look.

'What's the Taj done to upset you?' he repeated.

'It's a tomb!' Tara said defensively. 'Besides, I've already seen it.'

It had been a hateful trip, staying in a cheap hotel and going to the Taj on a bus full of other penny-pinching small-town tourists. Seeing the Taj with Vikram would be something else all together—but visiting a monument to love when they were both marrying for convenience seemed ironic to say the least.

'Hmm,' he said thoughtfully. 'I'll figure something else out, then.' He touched her hair, threading his fingers slowly through its length. 'Let me know what you want to do about your surname.'

'I'd like to keep my own, if it's all the same to you,' Tara said. 'I don't like the sound of Naintara Krishnan.'

She stood up abruptly. The feel of his hands tangling in her hair was doing weird things to her insides, and the temptation to jump on him and claw his clothes off was immense. But both their mothers were in the next room. Being caught making out with her fiancé in the living room of her parents' house would give bringing shame to the family a completely new and different twist.

'Something wrong?' Vikram asked when she got up and moved away.

'No,' Tara replied. 'I'm tired of sitting in one place like a lump of dough, that's all.'

He grinned at that, lounging back on the cushions. 'You don't look very doughy,' he said. 'More like a jumpy kitten. Come back here.'

There wasn't even a hint of command in his voice, but Tara found herself obeying him automatically, going and sitting next to him on the sofa.

'Nervous about the honeymoon?' he asked softly, and she nodded.

'It's not just the honeymoon, it's the whole marriage thing!' she blurted out. 'It's taking on a life of its own. My mum is obsessing about my trousseau, yours is picking out honeymoon destinations, there's a bunch of my dad's relatives coming down from Chennai I've never met before in my life. I've completely lost track of what's happening! And I'm finding it difficult to get my head around the whole thought of being married. This isn't like going away to college, is it? It's like a…a…brand-new life I'm getting into, and I don't feel prepared. You seem so completely in control, and you know exactly what you want. I feel like a confused mess in comparison!' She ran out of breath and stopped.

'I'm a little nervous, too,' he said quietly.

She blinked. 'Are you?' she asked, 'Seriously?'

Vikram's voice had a wry undertone as he replied. 'Seriously. I guess I'm just better at hiding it than you are.'

'Lawyer training.' Tara sighed. 'Playing your cards close to your chest. I wish someone had taught *me* how to do that. I inevitably say exactly what I'm thinking.'

'That's one of the nicest things about you,' Vikram said, and smiled. 'Don't look so tragic, Tara, it'll work out. We're both sensible people, and each of us knows what the other one is expecting from this marriage. There's no reason for things to go wrong.'

Put like that, their wedding sounded like a dry and soulless business arrangement. Tara sighed again. She'd told Vikram she didn't believe in romance and being swept off her feet, but a small dose of affection would have helped.

Vikram watched her square her shoulders uncon-sciously, as if to prepare for a not very palatable task. Her smooth forehead was puckered in thought, and her lips were pursed slightly. She looked determined and vulnerable at the same time. So far he'd been very careful not to touch her, beyond a casual peck on the cheek or a caress on the hand, but the temptation to kiss her now was immense.

'You're leaving tomorrow, aren't you?' Tara asked, her head still downcast.

'I've been away from work for almost two weeks,' Vikram said. 'I need to get back and get things in order before November.'

Tara didn't reply, and he took her chin between his thumb and forefinger, tipping her face up so that he could look into her eyes.

'Cheer up,' he said quietly.

She blinked, a little breathless, 'I am! I mean I'm cheerful enough. Just a little jittery.'

'Maybe this will help...' he said.

She shivered at the promise in his husky voice, staring mesmerised into his eyes as he bent his head. He kissed her very gently, his lips feather-light against hers. The sensation was exquisite, but Tara felt herself begin to panic. She didn't know how to respond. Her impulse was to drag his head closer and make him keep kissing her, but she had a feeling she should be doing something herself—moving her lips? Doing something with her tongue? She could have screamed in frustration when he released her after barely ten seconds.

'See you in a month,' he said softly, and she stepped back.

They didn't have much time to talk after that, as Vikram's mother came bustling into the room after a few minutes to take Tara's opinion on a menu for the wedding reception.

* * *

The next month was crazy. Vikram went back to Bengaluru after putting an embarrassingly large diamond on Tara's finger, and both his mother and Tara's threw themselves into wedding preparations. Tara stayed out of them as much as possible, concentrating on getting some preliminary reading done for her PhD before the wedding took over her life. Vikram called a few times, and e-mailed often, but the conversations had a surreal quality to them—they ended up discussing trivial things, like whether the colour of the tie he was wearing to the reception would clash with her sari, rather than the fact that they were days away from committing to spending the rest of their lives together.

The wedding itself was to be a quiet family affair—Vikram wanted it that way, and Tara's father had reluctantly agreed. Tara felt a bit of a fraud as her mother carefully arranged the folds of her green and gold brocade sari.

The whole thing didn't seem real yet, she thought, moving her head irritably. In addition to the weight of her already heavy hair, she had enough flowers pinned in it to stock a moderate-sized florist's shop for a week. She was extremely sleep-deprived—she hadn't slept much the night before, and the ceremony was starting at an unearthly hour in the morning because that was the 'auspicious time' the Krishnans' priest had come up with. And she was very, very jittery.

The enormity of what she was doing had just begun to dawn on her, and the result was as fine an attack of nerves as one could have hoped for.

'This'll be your first night—' her mother started to say.

Tara cut across her rudely. 'If you're going to tell me the facts of life, Mum, you're some ten years too late.' Her mother flushed painfully, sending Tara into one of her instant guilt trips. 'Sorry, Amma,' she muttered.

Her mother recovered with dignity. 'It'll still be your first time. If you need to know something, ask me.'

'Yeah, right…' Tara muttered to herself.

Her mother hadn't even bothered to tell her about contraception—if she thought her daughter was all that innocent, wouldn't that be the least she'd do? Or maybe she *wanted* her to get pregnant, Tara thought darkly, so that she'd give up all hopes of having a career, or even a life of her own. Anyway, she'd sorted things out for herself, going to the gynaecologist mother of a friend of hers and getting three months' supply of the Pill.

She was still brooding when her closest friend, Ritu, entered the room.

'I'll take over, Aunty,' she said cheerfully to Tara's mum. 'Only the make-up to be done, right?'

Tara's mother escaped thankfully, and Ritu pulled up a chair.

'Nervy?' she asked, raising her eyebrows.

Tara nodded.

'I take back everything I said about this being a bad idea.' Ritu said. 'I saw your fiancé for about five minutes outside, and he's gorgeous. Most women would kill for a night with a man like that.'

Tara gulped. Other than a kissing session with a college classmate, which she'd entered into on a purely experimental basis, she was terribly inexperienced when it came to men. And Vikram looked anything but inexperienced. He'd probably slept with dozens of women. The thought of the wedding night had her tied up in knots. She was so unsure about what to do and how to behave. The thought of actually getting into bed with Vikram was scary and exciting at the same time, and a little shiver went through her.

'Feeling cold?' Ritu asked, oblivious to the turmoil in her best friend's mind. 'It'll be warmer in the main hall—it's actually getting a bit stuffy. There are dozens of people around. You sure you don't have some gate-crashers in there?'

Tara grinned unwillingly. At some point, the 'quiet family affair' had got completely out of control, probably because the 'family' on either side numbered over a hundred people. The noise filtered in even through the closed doors of the changing room. Everyone was talking and laughing at once, the priest was chanting Sanskrit mantras at the top of his voice, and to add to the pandemonium there were live musicians playing traditional music to accompany the mantras. The plaintive strains of the *nadaswaram* in the background intensified the fluttery feeling in Tara's stomach, and for an instant she had a childish impulse to cover her ears with her hands.

After about ten more minutes her mother turned up again, to lead her out to the wedding pavilion.

'I can't see—stop shoving me!' she hissed, her eyes discreetly lowered as her mother had instructed.

She was seething as she was finally pushed into her seat in front of the sacred fire by various over-helpful female relatives. The noise was much louder, and the heavy beat of the drum seemed to make her heart pound harder.

Her eyes began to water—the priest had just poured a pot of butter into the fire, and it was smoking dreadfully.

'Such a coincidence, meeting you here,' an extremely sexy voice drawled into her ear.

She spun towards the sound and found herself looking right into Vikram's eyes.

'Calm down,' he said, lowering his voice. 'Not changed your mind, have you? You look more like you're at a funeral than a wedding.'

'I feel ridiculously over-dressed,' Tara muttered, taking in the sight of Vikram in a white T-shirt over a *veshti,* the single white cotton kilt-like lower garment that was traditional male garb for any South Indian religious occasion—weddings and funerals included.

His hair was still damp from the shower, and the white collar of his T-shirt set off his tanned skin to perfection. Ritu was right—he looked gorgeous. Tara unconsciously clenched her hands. It wasn't *fair.* She didn't want to be attracted to him so strongly. He was just looking at her now, for God's sake, and it was driving her crazy with longing. The suppressed heat in his eyes was making her imagine all kinds of delicious things.

'You look absolutely stunning,' he said finally, his voice low. 'Don't look at him now, but even the *pundit's* checking you out.'

Tara smiled. She couldn't help it. Vikram was perhaps a little too calm and collected, but he definitely was a help in getting things into perspective.

'That's better,' Vikram said. 'I feel a little less like an undertaker's assistant now.'

She laughed at that, and both her parents gave her disapproving looks.

'Vikram, *kannan,* you can't get married wearing a T-shirt,' one of the hovering aunts clicked in exasperation.

In addition to the *veshti,* tradition also dictated a bare-chested dress code for men.

'It's cold,' someone else said chidingly. 'He can take the T-shirt off once the actual ceremonies begin.'

'They're about to begin!' the first voice chimed in. 'Vikram…'

'Yes—OK!' he said in exasperation, and stood up, pulling the T-shirt over his head in one fluid movement.

Ohhhh. He had the best body Tara had ever seen off-screen, and she almost cried out in protest when he slung an *angavastram* carelessly across one shoulder, the white cloth covering up a large part of his near-perfect chest.

'Drool alert,' Ritu whispered warningly into her ear.

Tara looked away in a hurry, hoping none of the aunts had noticed her casting lustful looks at her almost-husband. She couldn't turn off the images in her mind, though—her anticipation for their first night together had just been turned up a notch.

Most of the ceremony passed by in blur—except for her having to perch on Vikram's knee for the duration of one particularly complex ritual. In her efforts to a) not put her full weight on him, and b) not seem too flustered at having to climb onto his lap in front of a hundred interested onlookers, she almost overbalanced.

He put his hands around her waist, his warm palms touching her bare skin just above the waistband of the sari. 'Relax, you won't crush me,' he said, and pulled her back against him.

Tara sat quietly, doing her best not to breathe. For

the few minutes she stayed on his lap she felt as if they were isolated from the rest of the world. The priest's chants and the excited conversation among their relatives seemed to be coming from a long, long distance away. All that was real was the feeling of his hands on her waist, and his breath on the nape of her neck. She had a sudden mad urge to turn around and press her lips to his, and she almost shuddered with the effort of keeping still.

Finally the priest beamed around at everyone, pronouncing all the ceremonies done, and the magistrate's assistant came forward with the marriage register. Tara felt her heart thumping in her chest as she signed it. This was it. She was tied to Vikram for the rest of her life now. She caught her father wiping his eyes furtively and was almost unbearably touched. Her mother, in contrast, for once looked completely in control.

'So far, so good,' Vikram murmured out of the corner of his mouth as they posed for photographs with the nth set of beaming relatives. 'Are you feeling better now? For a minute I thought you'd bolt—you looked petrified.'

'I didn't!' Tara said indignantly. Talk about a mood-killer. 'It was all that smoke and noise.'

'Smoke and noise?' he repeatedly thoughtfully. 'Hmm…'

His arm slipped round her waist, and he bent and lightly brushed his lips against hers. It was a teasingly casual embrace, but her already heightened senses went haywire at his touch. She instinctively leaned into the kiss, blushing when he drew away and surveyed her with amused eyes.

'I'm looking forward to tonight,' he said huskily, almost to himself.

Someone called out to him, but he held her gaze for a few seconds, his jet-black eyes burning into hers before he turned away. Tara could feel her pulse racing. Thankfully no one was near enough to notice her agitation, and she took a couple of deep breaths before she went to stand by Vikram's side for the next round of photographs.

CHAPTER THREE

TARA scowled into the mirror. 'This blouse was a mistake,' she said, looking at the fussy red and silver long-sleeved brocade blouse she was supposed to wear for the wedding reception that Vikram's father was hosting at his swanky club. 'I shouldn't have let my mother and the tailors bulldoze me into getting it stitched this way. I look ridiculous.'

'Tara, it's too late to do anything. The guests have begun to arrive,' Ritu protested. 'Put it on, and we'll drape the sari in a way so it doesn't look too bad.'

'I am *not* about to step out in front of a thousand people dressed like Santa Claus in drag,' Tara said through her teeth. 'Can you get me a pair of scissors from somewhere?'

'Tara…' Ritu said despairingly.

Tara turned around. 'I need to look like I belong with Vikram,' she said. 'Not like some schoolroom miss dressed up by her mum.'

Ritu's face softened. 'Right,' she said. 'Let's do what we can.'

Twenty minutes later Vikram looked up as a slim figure dressed in a sari crossed the club lawns gracefully to come towards him. It took him a few seconds to recognise his wife. Her thick hair was piled into a beehive hairdo that left her long, graceful neck exposed, and her sari was a light-coloured shimmery thing that made her look like a moonbeam. But it wasn't the sari everyone around him was staring at—it was the blouse.

At first glance it looked as if she wasn't wearing one at all, as if the only thing covering her breasts was the gauzy material of the sari that crossed from her right hip to flow over her left shoulder. Closer inspection showed that she *was* wearing a blouse—a thin strip of material that barely covered her breasts and was tied in a knot at her back. Most of her back was bare, Vikram noticed as she came to stand beside him. So was most of her waist. The sari was tied very low, and her navel peeped out seductively above the point where the front pleats were tucked into the waistband of the satin underskirt.

A sharp wave of lust hit Vikram just below his belly as a vivid mental image of slowly pulling the sari off sprang up. He took a quick swig of his drink to regain his composure, and held his hand out to Tara. 'You look lovely,' he said, smiling at her warmly.

Tara tucked a hand into the crook of Vikram's arm. For the second before Vikram had smiled she had been on tenterhooks. Between her efforts and Ritu's the blouse had ended up a good deal skimpier than she'd intended. It wasn't indecent, but it definitely didn't suggest a virginal bride, and she'd been worried that Vikram would disapprove.

Vikram put an arm around her and steered her to the next group of guests. Acutely conscious of the strength cloaked under the silk sleeve of his jacket, she was glad of the arm for another reason—she was beginning to feel very, very cold. It was evening, and around fifteen degrees Celsius, and they were right out in the open. She gave a little involuntary shiver as a gust of cold wind blew across the lawns.

'Do you want to go inside?' Vikram asked.

She nodded, hoping her teeth wouldn't begin to chatter. Indoors would be warmer, and she desperately wanted to be alone with him—not standing around and socialising with a bunch of their parents' friends. He was looking good enough to eat. This was the first time she'd seen him in a suit and tie, and he was gorgeous, the perfectly cut suit emphasising the powerful breadth of his shoulders and the white shirt setting off his smoothly tanned skin. His straight black hair flopped over his forehead, and he kept pushing it back impatiently with one hand.

For a moment Tara wondered what the reaction of the assembled guests would be if she leaned across and planted a passionate kiss on his beautiful mouth. Yet another twist to bringing shame on the family if she did. Vikram might end up being the only Indian man in history having to fight off public advances from his newly acquired bride. Sighing, she allowed Vikram to lead her inside the main hall, where a buffet dinner had been laid out.

It *was* warmer inside, but not much, and Vikram frowned as he felt her icy hands. 'Drink this, it'll warm you up,' he said, stopping a passing waiter to grab a bowl of soup.

Tara took it from him gratefully, cupping her slim hands around the bowl to soak in the warmth.

Ritu spotted her and came across. 'Here—I got you a wrap,' she said, thrusting a silvery-white hand-embroidered Pashmina shawl into her hand. 'It's a wedding gift from one of your aunts,' she said, when Tara looked up at her enquiringly. 'I heard her twittering on about how well it would have matched your sari, so I dug it out and unwrapped it. *You* have a matching tie,' she said, turning to Vikram. 'I left it in the box. Now, get this girl to cover up before she freezes to death.'

Vikram looked after Ritu as she bustled off. 'I like your friend,' he observed, and Tara found herself liking him even more.

Without realising it, she started telling him the story of the mutilated blouse, and he laughed, his black eyes sparkling with amusement. He was still laughing when a tall woman with restless eyes wandered up to them. Tara had spotted her earlier, standing alone by the bar. She was really lovely, in a film actressy kind of way, and she was dressed in an expensive-looking *churidaar kameez* that proclaimed designer-wear from a mile off.

Vikram's expression changed, becoming almost sombre the second he saw her. 'Tara, this is Lisa Andrews—a very close friend of ours,' he said as he stood up to greet her.

The girl leaned across to kiss Tara on the cheek, surprising her so much that she only just managed to stop herself from jerking back. People in Jamshedpur normally shook hands—kissing on the cheek was a western custom that was only slowly coming into vogue in society circles of big cities.

Lisa was smiling, taking her hands into her own. 'You're beautiful,' she said.

Her voice was so genuinely warm that Tara abandoned the thought that she might be an ex-girlfriend.

'I'm so happy Vikram's finally married. We were beginning to give up on him.' She looked up at Vikram and smiled. 'He's a wonderful person. You're a really lucky girl,' she said, and squeezed Tara's hands once gently before letting them go. She kissed Vikram next, and hugged him briefly. 'Congratulations, and I hope you'll be really, really happy,' she said.

But there was something in her eyes—a lurking sadness that made Tara feel strangely uncomfortable. Her eyes followed Lisa as she walked away, and she saw Vikram's mother hurry up to her and put an arm around her. There was something happening here, Tara thought, and she looked up at Vikram. He was looking at the two women, too, and there was a kind of frozen look on his face that made the question Tara was about to ask die on her lips.

Then another set of people came up, and Vikram turned to greet them—he sounded so normal that Tara began to wonder if she'd been imagining things.

They finally had dinner at eleven o' clock, after all the guests had left. Then the two of them, plus both sets of parents, were taken to the Krishnans' bungalow in three different chauffeur-driven cars.

After much discussion on whether their first night should be at a hotel or in the Krishnans' home, it had finally been decided by the powers that be that Vikram's parents' home was the best place for Tara to lose her virginity.

Being escorted there by her own parents was embarrassing beyond belief, and as far as she knew *not* part of tradition, but she hadn't had the guts to put her foot down. Vikram seemed completely unfazed, she thought, peeking at his face quickly as they entered the house. Maybe the first night wasn't quite such a big thing for him—again she told herself he'd probably slept with dozens of women. Of course he hadn't married any of them, but he'd still find *her* totally inexperienced in comparison.

A maid showed Tara to the room she'd be sharing with Vikram. It was lovely, and someone had strewn the bed with rose-petals. Tara repressed a grimace, looking at it. It so obviously screamed out *wedding night bed.* Her cases were already in the room, ready to be carried to the station the next day, and once the maid had left she quickly changed into a demure but alluring white satin nightgown, with narrow pink shoulder-straps and pale pink rosebuds embroidered over the bodice.

After the episode with the sari earlier in the evening she thought it better to be conservative with her night clothes, at least in the beginning. The nightgown had a matching robe, and she slipped it on—in spite of the heater in the room it was still a little chilly—then she carefully brushed the rose petals off one side of the bed and sat herself down to wait.

Her anticipation had built up to fever-pitch by the time Vikram entered the room, and her uncertainties were beginning to build as well. She had no idea what he expected of her. He must know how inexperienced she was, and he might be put off if she acted too eager. On the other hand he didn't seem the kind of man who'd appreciate a shy and blushing bride, and in any case she wasn't sure she could manage pretending to be one.

God, this was crazy. The simplest thing would be to

ask the man, admit openly that ever since she'd clapped eyes on him she'd been lusting after his body. She didn't have a clue what to do about it. Asking him would probably violate about a dozen traditions, and might even reflect badly on the way she'd been brought up. A little too late she wished she'd allowed her mother to give her the first night talk. It might have included some useful tips on etiquette.

Tara peeked up at Vikram. He looked devastatingly handsome, but entirely too large and intimidating. She put the last lingering thought of asking him anything firmly out of her mind. He was still wearing the suit he had worn to the reception, and he shrugged the jacket off to cast it negligently over a chair. Tara's eyes involuntarily went to the neck of his white silk shirt as he took off his tie and loosened the top two buttons.

'Tired?' he asked as he sat down in an elaborately carved armchair next to the bed.

Tara shook her head, studiously looking down at her nails. He leaned back in the chair, lazily surveying her through hooded eyes. Tara was beginning to feel a bit like an exhibit in a zoo.

He held an arm out and said, 'Come here.'

His voice held a caressing note that was unfamiliar and almost impossible to resist. Tara got off the bed and went to him, and he drew her onto his knee, pulling her back so that her head rested comfortably under his chin. Her hair was still done up in its elaborate bun, and he started drawing the pins out gently, one by one, so that her hair tumbled down around her shoulders.

'Beautiful,' he said, his voice a little huskier than normal.

His hands were gentle, caressing her face and then her upper arms as he bent to kiss her lips gently. The sensation was as exquisite as it had been the first time he kissed her, but Tara found it difficult to respond, jerking away involuntarily when his hands wandered a little lower. He took his hands away immediately, putting his arms around her instead so that he held her close. She could hear the steady thump of his heartbeat, and she found the sound oddly reassuring.

They stayed that way for a few minutes, and then he tipped up her face and kissed her again, his lips more demanding this time, his body pressed up very close to hers. Tara gave herself completely to the sensation, shuddering with pleasure as he slid the straps of her nightdress off her shoulders to press hot kisses over her throat and breasts. His hands were stroking over her waist and hips, and with an incoherent little sound Tara began to return his kisses, clumsily undoing the buttons of his shirt to tug the material away and expose a broad expanse of tanned, hair-roughened chest.

The problem was she didn't really know what to do next. He was moving too fast for her. Her nightdress was already pooled around her waist, and as he moved her in his arms to slip it off completely she whimpered in protest.

Vikram drew away again, and she quickly tugged up the straps of the nightdress, not daring to look him in the face. She was trembling now, partly in reaction and partly in embarrassment.

Vikram's hands came up to frame her face. 'Nervous?' he asked softly.

She nodded. Even her hands were shaking now. Quite naturally Vikram assumed she was scared.

'Don't worry. It doesn't have to be tonight,' he said gently. 'Lie down and get some sleep if you want. I'll move to the sofa.'

'There's a lot's of space in the bed,' she ventured, wondering how to make it clear that, nervous or not, she was quite ready for some action.

Vikram smiled wryly. 'I think that would be a little too much for my self-control,' he said, leaning across and snapping the light off.

Tara stayed awake, staring quietly at the ceiling. This was a bit of an anti-climax. She *had* been nervous—still was—but she hadn't expected him to back off quite so readily. A little bit of attempted seduction would have been more than fine by her. New worries began to assail her. Didn't he find her attractive enough? Had she ruined everything by acting gauche and immature?

Being married was turning out to be a lot more complicated than she'd thought, and she pulled herself together with an effort. 'Vikram?' she said in a small voice, wondering how to get him back into bed without coming across like a nymphomaniac.

'Mmm?' he replied.

She suppressed a little flurry of annoyance. He could have at least said yes at least instead of grunting at her. Then again, he was probably half asleep.

'Um, can I change my mind?'

CHAPTER FOUR

SEVERAL hours later, Tara rolled over in bed and drew the covers around her a little more closely. So far the night had been the most interesting one in her short life. She looked up at Vikram, who'd propped himself up on one elbow and was gently trailing a finger down her cheek.

'Was it very bad?' he asked.

She shook her head. 'It hurt like blazes in the beginning, that's all,' she said, and buried her face in his shoulder. 'I was awful, wasn't I?'

All she could think was that he'd now be comparing her unfavourably with every other woman he'd ever been with—probably even regretting marrying her.

Vikram's hand paused for a second, and then continued on its way down her bare shoulder. 'No, you weren't,' he said, kissing the nape of her neck. 'Tonight was probably one of the best nights of my life. I only wish it had been better for you.'

So, all right, he wasn't complaining. But he might still be comparing. Tara peered at him in the dark, trying to make out his expression. But it was impossible—he was just a black hulking silhouette. She hadn't let him put on a night light because she'd been embarrassed, and the only light in the room came from outside.

The room they were in faced towards the steel factory where both their fathers worked, and the night sky blazed with light every time a load of slag was dumped out of the huge furnace. An almost perfectly timed flash lit up the room at that point. Filtered through the curtains, the light was a pale unearthly orange, lighting up the planes and angles of Vikram's face. His usually rather hard expression had been replaced by something that was almost tender, Tara noted. And his torso, as the glimpse she'd got during the wedding had promised, was amazing.

'Maybe I need practice?' she ventured finally, doing her best to keep her voice from squeaking as his hand burrowed under the covers.

'Practice will help,' he agreed solemnly. 'Lots of it, preferably. You can count on me.'

The room was almost completely dark now, and Tara welcomed him with open arms as he bent to cover her lips with his.

Waking up the next morning was tough. Tara felt a large hand shaking her shoulder and burrowed even further down under the covers. 'Not morning yet,' she muttered.

'Should I get you breakfast in bed?' Vikram asked.

Her eyes flew open as she realised where she was. 'Damn,' she said, sitting up, careful to keep the covers around her. It was evidently past nine, and she blushed at the thought of having to go out and face knowing looks from the rest of the household.

Vikram had been up for a while, evidently—his hair was damp from the shower and he was wearing jeans and a T-shirt. The muscles in his shoulders and chest strained against the thin material of the T-shirt as he moved, and Tara felt her mouth suddenly go dry.

'I'll give you a few minutes to yourself,' Vikram said. 'Will you be able to find your way to the dining room?'

It wasn't a facetious question—the bungalow was large, and had several interlinked verandas and corridors that it would be easy to lose one's way in.

'I'll manage,' Tara said, waiting until he left the room before she got out of bed and ran across the room to bolt the door behind him.

Her body ached in unfamiliar places, but her lips curved up in a smile. So far, so good, she thought. Vikram had turned out to be a surprisingly gentle and considerate lover—and she'd been right. All she'd needed was some more practice. She was positively looking forward to the honeymoon now.

Meeting Vikram's parents on the 'morning after' turned out to be less embarrassing than she'd thought it would be—they were both acting perfectly normal, with no knowing looks, and neither of them asked her if she'd slept well.

'I'm sorry we didn't wait for you,' Mr Krishnan said, smiling at her across the breakfast table. 'Vikram wasn't sure how long you'd take, and I need to leave for work in little while.'

'You work way too hard,' Mrs Krishnan scolded. 'You could have taken the day off. No wonder Vikram works the crazy hours he does with you for an example.'

'Compared to Vikram, I barely work,' Mr Krishnan said drily. 'We should all count ourselves lucky that it's not *him* rushing off to work the day after his wedding.'

Mrs Krishnan frowned. 'That will all change now that he's married,' she said. 'Tara will make sure he gets home on time every day.'

'Assuming she wants me home on time every day,' Vikram said.

Tara barely restrained herself from saying that she didn't care what hours he kept as long as he was home at night.

'Of course she does,' Mrs Krishnan said, and gave Tara an affectionate pat on the hand. 'We're really lucky to have you in the family. Vijay would have been so thrilled... He used to tease Vikram all the time, saying no one would want to marry a lawyer.'

There was a short silence, and Tara was about to ask who Vijay was when she looked across at Mrs Krishnan. She was sitting very still, her plate untouched in front of her, as tears slowly welled up in her eyes. Mr Krishnan got up and gently put his arm around her.

'Vyjanthi,' he said warningly. 'Don't start getting depressed now.'

Mrs Krishnan nodded and made a valiant attempt to control her expression, moving the tea things around the table and not looking up. Then her face crumpled, and she muttered, 'I'm sorry...' She hurried out of the room.

Vikram put down his coffee cup and went after her, leaving Tara and Mr Krishnan looking at each other.

'I'm so sorry, my dear,' Mr Krishnan said, recovering first and patting Tara's arm awkwardly. 'Do excuse my wife. The strain's been a bit too much for her. Ever since Vijay... It's been very difficult for her.'

He evidently expected her to know who Vijay was,

and Tara wasn't sure how to break it to him that she didn't have a clue.

Vikram returned a few minutes later. 'Mum's lying down,' he said in answer to his father's enquiring look. 'She's completely wrung out. She wanted to come back and say goodbye to Tara before we leave, but I said I'd apologise on her behalf.'

Mr Krishnan sighed heavily. 'I'll go to her,' he said. 'Have a good trip, both of you.' He shook hands with Vikram and gave Tara a fatherly pat on the head before he left the room in search of his wife.

'We should leave in half an hour,' Vikram said, not looking at Tara. 'The trip to Pench is going to be pretty tiring.'

'I'll go and get ready, then,' Tara replied, and then, tentatively, 'Vikram…why was your mum so upset?'

'I'm sorry. I should have told you,' Vikram said, his voice stiff. 'I had a younger brother who died in an accident three years ago. My mother's not over it fully yet.'

He turned towards her, and Tara's instinctively sympathetic response died in her throat when she saw the rigid expression on his face. It was as if the Vikram she thought she knew had suddenly been whisked away, to be replaced by an emotionless stranger.

'I'll carry the cases out,' he was saying, his voice perfectly controlled. 'Maybe you could just check in the room that there's nothing you've left behind?'

Tara nodded, her head in a whirl. Granted, they'd not spent too much time together—but a brother she didn't even know about? Shouldn't Vikram have mentioned him at some point? His parents obviously talked about him quite freely, but she'd spent even less time with them than she had with Vikram. She'd even said something to him once about both of them being only children, and he hadn't bothered to contradict her.

Vikram watched her leave the room and his jaw tightened. He'd been stupid, not telling her about Vijay, but the topic wasn't one you could bring up easily in a regular conversation. She'd have questions now, and they'd be even more difficult to answer than if he'd just told her about Vijay earlier.

It was late evening before they reached the tiger reserve in Pench, and Tara was exhausted. They'd crossed half the country—first driving from Jamshedpur to Kolkata, catching a flight to Nagpur, and then driving for another three hours to reach Pench. Vikram had been silent for most of the journey, other than checking with her at regular intervals to make sure she was comfortable. Tara had been uncharacteristically quiet as well. Everything she'd tried to say had come out sounding either overly self-conscious or overly formal, and she'd soon stopped trying, burying herself in a book.

Halfway between Nagpur and Pench Tara had drifted off to sleep, the book slipping from her fingers. Vikram had picked it up and put it into her handbag. She'd looked adorable as she slept, her long eyelashes fanning out against her smooth pink cheeks. The road had been bumpy, and he'd put an arm around her to steady her, his heart quickening a little at the trustful way she snuggled up to him.

He was acutely aware of the barrier that had come up between them ever since she'd found out about Vijay, but he couldn't see what he could do about it. His brother's death was like a raw, open wound, and he couldn't bear talking about it—not to anyone. Tara must have sensed his discomfort because she hadn't asked any questions after his terse explanation of his mother's breakdown. The incident had cast a shadow on both of them, though, and a wariness had crept into Tara's conversation that hadn't been there before.

Tara had woken up a few seconds before they reached Pench, sitting up straight and stretching herself like a little cat.

'Dinner first,' she said now, when the receptionist at the luxury jungle lodge asked her if they wanted to be shown to their bungalow. 'I'm starving.'

Vikram nodded, and after asking for their luggage to be delivered to their room, he followed her into the small dining room. There was a buffet dinner laid out, and he filled his plate before joining her at the table. She frowned at it as he sat down.

'You eat meat?' she asked.

Vikram looked down at his plate. 'Yes, I believe I do,' he said slowly. 'Is that a problem?'

Tara put down her soup spoon. 'Of course not!' she said. 'Don't be so prickly. I assumed you'd be vegetarian because your parents are, that's all. And you ordered vegetarian food the night we went out for dinner in Jamshedpur.'

'It was a vegetarian restaurant,' he pointed out, and she laughed.

'Oh, of course—I didn't realise.' She looked at him curiously for a bit. 'I don't know anything about you, do I?'

His food preferences were a minor matter, but she still felt disturbed when she thought of his mother breaking down after the wedding. This wasn't the right time to ask about his brother, though.

Vikram shrugged. 'We haven't spent much time together. We'll find things out as we go along, I guess.'

He gently ran a finger down her arm, and Tara felt a pleasurable little shiver run through her. She felt quite bereft when Vikram removed his hand and went back to his dinner. She could think more clearly when he wasn't touching her, though, and that was a definite plus.

'You know pretty much everything about me,' she pointed out. 'Right down to what size knickers I wear.'

Vikram looked up, an indefinable expression in his eyes. There was a pause before he spoke. 'Tara, I can see where this is coming from, but trust me—there isn't all that much to me. Let's just take things as they come. We're on our honeymoon. Let's enjoy the few days we have, and save the heavy conversations for later.'

Tara toyed with her food for a few seconds. 'Fair enough,' she said finally. 'So we treat the honeymoon like a holiday, then? Relax, eat lots of dessert, and have sex several times a day? Sounds like a plan.' She looked up in time to catch the look on Vikram's face, and burst into a spontaneous peal of laughter. 'Oh, God, that was a little too direct, wasn't it? Sorry. I just like getting things clear so that there's no confusion.'

'I've noticed,' Vikram said gravely, though a smile was tugging at the corners of his mouth. 'Yeah, that's pretty much what I meant.'

'Thought so,' Tara said. 'I'm fine with it—as long as we do get to talk when we're back.'

'We will,' he promised, his eyes softening as he looked at her. 'But, like I said, I don't have any dark secrets hidden away—it's just a question of us spending more time together.'

She had to be satisfied with that, though it still sounded as if he'd do his best to avoid any kind of soul-searching.

On the way out of the restaurant Vikram stopped by the receptionist's desk to figure out arrangements for the next day's safari. 'Carry on to the room,' he said to Tara. 'I'll join you in a bit.'

Tara gave him a disappointed look and went. She wanted him to come with her and make wild passionate love to her all night through, but she could hardly tell him that with a dozen people within earshot. In any case, he'd be along soon enough.

She brushed her teeth, and got into bed, trying to arrange herself in an alluring pose. Only it felt uncomfortable, and faintly ridiculous, so she sat up again. The fatigue of the journey was beginning to catch up with her, and she stifled a yawn as she set the alarm on her mobile for the safari the next morning. Wishing Vikram would hurry, she leaned back against the headboard and shut her eyes.

Vikram took longer than he'd expected—the hotel had needed copies of various documents from the forest department before they could be booked into the reserve— and it was past nine when he got back to the bungalow. Tara was snuggled up in bed, her lovely hair spread around her on the pillow. She was fast asleep.

The temptation to wake her up was almost irresistible—he was used to travelling, wasn't tired in the least, and he'd been looking forward to his second night with his wife. Especially after her saying that they should have sex several times a day. It didn't seem fair, though. She was very tired, and after all what was the hurry? He had the rest of his life to spend with her.

Ten minutes later, when he slid into bed next to her, she immediately scooted up to him, cuddling close. Vikram's body reacted enthusiastically and he turned towards her, hoping she'd woken up. She hadn't, but her movement pressed her against a very sensitive part of his anatomy and he groaned mentally. It was going to be a long and frustrating night.

The alarm rang stridently at four-thirty a.m., and Tara bounced out of bed almost immediately. 'Brr, it's cold,' she said, sliding her feet into slippers and grabbing a shawl to put around her shoulders. She was wearing a slightly more daring negligee than she had on her wedding night, and one black lace strap slipped to expose a delicately moulded shoulder.

'Do you want to skip the safari?' Vikram asked, his eyes on her bare shoulder.

'No,' Tara said firmly, pulling the strap up and winding the shawl around her more closely. 'The waiter told me that some people don't get to see a tiger even after six or seven safaris. I don't want to miss a single one.' She hadn't missed the look in his eyes, but she wanted to pay him back for not having woken her the previous night.

Damn the tigers, Vikram felt like saying. It had taken him a long while to get to sleep, and right now all he wanted to do was get Tara back into bed and make up for the time he'd lost the previous night. Tigers were all very well on the Discovery Channel—going out at five in the morning to see them was not his idea of honeymoon entertainment. Then he remembered Tara saying that all her life she'd wanted to see tigers in the wild, and he groaned and got out of bed. His plans for Tara would need to wait.

The Jeep was an open one, and even in three layers of warm clothing Tara felt half frozen by the time they got out of the lodge. The forest guide threw a couple of blankets into the back and she grabbed them up gratefully, handing one to Vikram and huddling into the second one.

'Still cold,' she said, her teeth rattling, 'It's freezing… my hands are turning to ice.'

Vikram put an arm out to pull her under his blanket. 'Hang on,' he said quietly and, unzipping his jacket under the blanket, put her hands against his chest. 'Better?'

Tara nodded. She could feel the buttons of his shirt under one hand and, feeling greatly daring, she undid one and slipped her hand in to rest against his bare skin. A shudder ran through his body—whether due to the cold or something else, she couldn't tell. She let her hands wander a little and heard his breath catch in his throat.

He grabbed her hand as it slid lower, and held it trapped against his chest. 'Wait till I get you alone,' he muttered threateningly into her ear, and Tara laughed a little.

Their Jeep took one of many trails into the jungle, and the forest guide started telling them about the animals and birds they could expect to see. Normally Tara would have been fascinated, but now she was barely listening, acutely conscious of the hard length of Vikram's body pressed against hers. Skipping the safari would have been an excellent idea, she thought confusedly as Vikram, holding both her hands trapped in one of his, gently slid his other hand under her top. All she could do was wriggle and gasp, and hope that neither the driver nor their guide decided to turn and look at them.

Vikram finally took pity on her when she started biting her lip and writhing against him. He removed his tormenting hand, putting it on her waist instead, and she gave a relieved little sigh. Then she found that she wanted the hand back where it had been a few seconds before. Her brain seemed to be getting scrambled after only one night of sex, she thought—she could think of nothing else. And all things considered the safari was turning out to be pretty much a waste of time. So far they'd seen a herd of deer, several monkeys and a few peacocks. Lots of birds. Not a single tiger. No wonder Vikram had wanted to stay back in the bungalow.

They drove on a little further and the driver braked abruptly, gesturing to them to stay silent. A bird screeched out a harsh alarm call and the herd of deer grazing by the side of the trail stiffened for a second, their ears perking up before they turned and bolted into the jungle.

Tara stood up in the Jeep, her hand on Vikram's shoulder as she peered down the trail. 'Look!' she mouthed at him, pointing at the massive tigress walking slowly down the trail towards them. Two almost fully-grown cubs followed her, and the three of them were breathtaking. There was no other word for it.

Tara sat down and clutched at Vikram's sleeve as they came closer. In her head she knew there was no danger, but the sheer size and strength of the animals made her feel very glad she had Vikram next to her.

The tigress and her cubs crossed the trail behind them, giving them a disdainful look before disappearing into the jungle. Tara sank back into her seat, her face still glowing with excitement. 'That was amazing, wasn't it?' she breathed.

For a single ludicrous second Vikram found himself feeling jealous of the tigers. 'I'm glad we didn't miss the safari,' he said, and a sudden surge of affection filled him as he looked at her vibrantly alive little face.

It struck him that it had been a long time since he had seen someone look so genuinely happy. At work everyone was under pressure all the time, and the people he socialised with weren't exactly Pollyannas, either. And his family... A sombre expression crossed his face. His parents had started smiling and laughing again, but he hadn't seen them look truly happy even once in the three years since Vijay's death.

The Jeep pulled up in a large clearing where a dozen or more other Jeeps were parked. The driver started unpacking breakfast, and Tara and Vikram got out of the vehicle to stretch their limbs. The sun had come out, and it was a lot warmer now. Tara discarded her heavy jacket. The driver got them steaming cups of tea and Tara sipped at hers a little too early, scalding her lips. She scowled, and Vikram tipped up her face gently to kiss her mouth gently. The Jeep shielded them from view, and Tara leaned closer into the kiss. Vikram took the cup from her and set it on the seat, continuing to kiss her all the while. They broke apart only when they ran out of breath.

'Should we get back to the hotel?' Vikram asked softly, and Tara nodded.

Neither of them spoke on the drive back. They'd cut the half-day safari short by more than two hours, but the driver and the guide had both given them understanding looks. Tara's brand-new *thaali* gave away her newly married status and, as the guide said later, a woman was a bride only once.

Back at the lodge, Tara's hands trembled as she tried to unlock the door to their bungalow. She got it open finally, and was barely inside before Vikram shut the door roughly with his foot, bolted it behind him, and picked her up to carry her to bed.

The next two days were bliss. They skipped most of the safaris, only going for one more on an afternoon when they held hands all the way and didn't see anything more exciting than deer and monkeys. Tara spent a few hours in the spa, and they swam every afternoon, but other than that they were in the room most of the time, discovering new and exciting things to do in bed. They skipped a lot of meals, too, ordering in room service whenever they felt hungry and raiding the mini-bar.

'So, where are we going next?' Tara asked curiously for about the tenth time when they'd checked out of the hotel on the third day. Vikram had been resolutely silent about their next destination, saying he wanted it to be a surprise.

Vikram laughed. 'We'll be there in an hour,' he said as he helped their driver load their luggage into the car. 'Wouldn't you rather wait till we get there?'

'No,' Tara said promptly. 'If you tell me now, and it

sounds awful, I have one hour in which to persuade you to change your mind.'

'Right,' Vikram said, getting into the car next to her and pulling her close. 'So it's this way. I have a friend from these parts—he's called Amar, you met him at our wedding reception. His grandparents were minor royalty, and his family still owns large tracts of land in the area. They've just got the *shikaarbadi,* the old hunting lodge, on one of their estates renovated. Eventually it'll be turned into a luxury hotel, and I've invested a fair bit in the renovation, hoping that the returns will be good. But right now it's a beautiful heritage home that's been restored to look exactly the way it did a hundred years ago—down to the furnishings and the paintings on the walls. It's by the side of a small lake, and the estate is heavily wooded. There's even a stream and a small waterfall. And the best part is that we've got it all to ourselves for the next week.' He broke off to give Tara a teasing look. 'You still want to turn back?'

'It sounds idyllic,' Tara said, her eyes aglow with excitement. 'I can hardly wait to see it.'

Vikram leaned down and kissed her impulsively. She put her arms around his neck, drawing him closer. A warning bell went off in his head. Tara was rapidly becoming an integral part of his existence, and he wasn't sure if that was a good thing. It was time he re-established the practical footing they'd started their marriage off on.

Gently he disengaged himself and said, 'There's a lot of history around the place, apparently.'

'Doomed lovers and duelling at dusk?' Tara suggested.

Vikram shook his head. 'Nothing that interesting. There was some fighting in the area during the 1857 war with the British, and I think a band of Indian rebels took refuge in the *shikaarbadi*. The Rajah at that time was a big supporter of the Indian freedom movement. And there are some ancient temple ruins from the 1600s. I'm not sure what the story around those is, but the caretaker's family has lived there for generations—they'll be able to tell us some more.'

'No ghosts?' Tara asked.

She sounded so hopeful that Vikram laughed, resisting the temptation to kiss her again. 'No ghosts,' he said. 'But if you like ghost stories the caretaker's your man. Look—we're nearly there.'

He pointed out of the window and Tara looked excitedly as the driver stopped the car and got out to open a massive wrought-iron gate. 'Have you been here before?' she asked.

'Once,' Vikram said, leaning forward to direct the driver to turn left where the rather bumpy lane they were on forked into two. 'That was a couple of years ago, though. Amar's had a lot of work done since then.'

The lane wound through the woods for a few hundred metres before it turned into a little clearing right in front of the *shikaarbadi*. Tara gasped in delight as she saw the lodge. It wasn't very large, but it was lovely—a weathered building in grey stone, with white latticed windows and bougainvillaea creepers covering most of one side.

'You can see the lake if you go around the house,' Vikram said as Tara slid out of the car. 'Or would you like to see inside the house first?'

'House first,' Tara decided, giving the woman who opened the door a friendly smile. She bowed in response, and Tara gave Vikram a startled look.

'Old family retainer,' Vikram said in an undertone. 'She's the caretaker's wife—tends to treat all Amar's friends as royalty as well.'

'Sounds medieval,' Tara said with a frown. 'Does Amar walk around with a sword by his side, twirling his moustache and calling for his dancing girls?'

Vikram tried to picture his extremely proper friend in the role of debauched royalty and his lips twitched. 'I don't think so,' he said. 'He's proud of his roots, which he has every right to be, but his fancy doesn't extend to dancing girls.'

Tara had stopped paying attention to what he was saying, though. She was looking at him very intently. 'You look so different when you smile,' she said abruptly. 'Years younger, and ever so much more attractive. Why are you so grim and serious most of the time?'

The second the words were out of her mouth she wished them back. Vikram's face had gone carefully expressionless, and he didn't say anything for several seconds.

Then he said lightly, 'The grim look is part of the lawyer package. Can't have my clients thinking I'm taking life too easy. Kamala's serving lunch in fifteen minutes—do you want to go freshen up?'

Tara went. Something had changed since they left Pench, she thought. Vikram was consciously holding back. He wasn't standoffish, exactly, but the easy rapport they'd shared over the last few days was gone. Looking at herself in the mirror, Tara grimaced. Maybe she'd read too much into the automatic closeness that came after sex, and he was trying to gently set things straight.

Vikram was scrolling through e-mails on his phone

when Tara rejoined him. 'Everything under control?' she ventured.

He gave her a perfunctory smile. 'Not really. There's a crisis brewing with one of my top clients. I'm sorry, Tara, but I might have to make a few calls later today.'

'Of course,' Tara said, though inwardly she wondered what kind of crisis could be important enough to interrupt their honeymoon.

Lunch was a well-cooked but largely silent meal. Vikram still seemed preoccupied with whatever was wrong at work, and he excused himself immediately afterwards and shut himself into the living room with his laptop and cell phone.

Left to herself, Tara spent the next few hours exploring the property. Kamala sent one of her daughters with Tara to show her around. The girl was bright and chatty, but Tara felt too dispirited to talk. She felt awful—as if she'd been abandoned halfway through her honeymoon. For the first time she began to have misgivings about Vikram. If he was like this on their honeymoon, what would he be like when he actually went back to work?

They had to turn back quite early—dusk fell quickly in the winter, and the woods were not very safe to wander around in after dark. Back in the lodge, Tara took a book out on to a veranda to read while she watched the sun set over the lake. The gentle to and fro motion of her swing seat had her almost falling asleep, and she jumped when the door behind her creaked open.

'Oh, it's you,' she said, subsiding back into the chair as Vikram stepped onto the veranda. 'I've been reading up on the history of this place. You were wrong, by the way,

I've come across two sets of doomed lovers in the book already, and I've only just reached the second chapter.'

'The author obviously knows his market,' Vikram said.

He sat down on the swing seat inches away from her, not touching, but still very, very close—so close that she could feel the warmth radiating from his body. Tara's senses immediately went on high alert. Unable to stop herself, she reached a hand out, lightly touching his arm. He was wearing a jacket and she ached to slide her hand under it, but felt too unsure of herself to try.

'Work done?' she asked.

Vikram didn't respond to her touch, but he didn't pull away, either. 'Done for today,' he said. 'My line of work can be maddening sometimes; it doesn't leave you with any kind of personal life.'

Not sure whether she should take the statement as an explanation or a warning, Tara stayed silent. The night was very quiet. Except for the chirring of a nameless but immensely annoying insect somewhere in the grass outside there wasn't a sound to be heard.

'This place is so peaceful,' Vikram said after a little while. 'Feels like a completely different world from Bengaluru.'

'It *is* a completely different world,' Tara said. 'I haven't seen a single human being apart from Kamala and her daughter the entire day. And the woods are really well preserved—your friend's done a fabulous job. It's like a conservation project, the way he's managed to re-do the place without disturbing the natural ecosystems in the least.'

Vikram turned to look at her lazily. 'Ah, I forgot you'd

be seeing it from a scientist's perspective. I believe Amar *did* take advice from an environmentalist group before he set about redoing the place. He spoke to me about it, and I thought it was a good idea—a project like this brings out every tree-hugger in the vicinity when it goes commercial. Having at least one major group taped up and on your side takes the wind out of their sails.'

Tara took her hand off his arm and sat up. 'That's a very cynical way of looking at it,' she said slowly. 'Is that really the way you think?'

No wonder he'd said she'd get to know him better when they'd spent more time together—this was a completely different side to him.

'Yes, it's exactly the way I think,' Vikram replied. 'And it's the way most businessmen think. If more NGOs realised it and played it to their advantage they'd achieve far more than they do through protest marches and hunger strikes.'

Tara frowned. 'It sounds all wrong,' she said.

'Why?'

'It's doing the right thing, but for the completely wrong reason!' she exclaimed. 'Like being faithful to your wife because alimony payments are expensive. Or donating money to charities so that you get a tax break. Or—'

'I get the picture,' Vikram interrupted. 'But, tell me, does the reason matter so long as the right thing gets done?'

Tara threw her hands up in exasperation. 'I give up,' she said. 'I'm terrible at counter-arguments—people used to walk all over me in school debating competitions. It'll take me till the middle of the night to think up a sensible rejoinder.'

'You could always wake me up,' Vikram said.

Tara shot him a quick look. The only light on the veranda was from two oil lamps mounted on the wall of the lodge, and she couldn't see his expression clearly—his head was thrown back against the cushions, and most of his face was in the shadows. Light fell on the strong brown column of his throat, and she could see the pulse beating at the base of it.

Her own throat went dry with desire, and she only just managed to mutter, 'Wake you up to explain why your point of view is irrational and wrong-headed?'

'Or for anything else you want,' he said, and she saw him smile slightly.

The smile was her undoing. She scooted along the seat till she was almost on his lap, and leaned over to kiss his lips hungrily. He put a hand up to hold her head against his, but otherwise didn't respond until she started unbuttoning his shirt, her fingers clumsy. Then he straightened up and pulled her swiftly onto his lap, whispering into her hair, 'I think we're going to be awake for a long, long while tonight.'

Tara gave a little gasp, and melted into his arms.

CHAPTER FIVE

'Put the pot of uncooked rice on the threshold,' Vikram's mother instructed over the phone.

'Right,' Vikram said through his teeth, vowing that this was the last time his parents would have a say in what he did.

Getting married was like giving them an unlimited license to interfere. It was only with great difficulty that he'd persuaded them not to come haring down to Bengaluru to welcome *his* wife into *his* home when they returned from their honeymoon. So far they had thankfully steered clear of his sex life, but he wouldn't put it past his mum to start reading out chapters of the Kamasutra to him just in case he didn't know what to do.

Tara stood patiently waiting for Vikram to finish setting things up. 'You can cross the threshold now,' he said finally. 'You need to knock the rice over when you step in.'

Tara thought back to the last movie in which she'd seen it done, and raised a graceful little foot to tip the pot over and step into the house.

Vikram sighed in relief. 'Done,' he reported into the phone. His mother started to say something, but he cut her off brusquely. 'Talk to you in a bit—I need to get the luggage in.'

He'd omitted the *aarti* he was supposed to do, but he'd forgotten about getting a *thaali* ready, and didn't even have matches or a lighter to light the lamp with. In any case, he had a distinct feeling that his mum had mixed the rituals up—the South Indian one involved large plates with turmeric and *sindoor* mixed in water. The rice thing was something she'd probably seen on TV.

Once inside the house, Tara looked around delight-edly. It was a large semi-detached, in a row of similar houses, but in a large city like Bengaluru where most people lived in flats it was luxury to have an independent house. The living-room décor was deceptively simple—white walls, a few pieces of austere-looking teakwood furniture, and a single large painting that dominated the room. Tara put her bag down on the dining table and walked across the room to look at the painting. It was an abstract, swirls of yellow and orange on white, and just looking at it lifted her spirits.

Vikram cleared his throat and she jumped guiltily.

'Art connoisseur?' he enquired drily.

Tara shook her head. 'I did an online art appreciation course once,' she admitted. 'Learnt very little, unfortu-nately. I like this—who's the artist?'

'A friend of mine, he said. 'Lisa. I don't know if you remember her? She came for the wedding.'

Tara nodded as Vikram picked up the cases and started walking towards the stairs. 'I thought she was an interior designer or something of that sort,' she said.

'She is,' Vikram said. 'She did the interiors for this house. Painting is something she does in her spare time.'

Tara was dying to ask him more about Lisa, but there was a note in Vikram's voice that stopped her from asking further questions. 'Do you want some tea?' she asked instead.

'That'd be nice,' he said. 'Green, please. There's a tin in the cupboard above the stove.'

The kitchen was state-of-the-art, and it took Tara a little while to figure things out. Vikram had finished carrying up the luggage and was in the living room doing something with the music system by the time she emerged.

'Thanks,' he said, taking the teacup from her. 'I think I need to get a sound engineer in to rewire the system. There's something off about it right now.' A strange expression crossed his face after he took a sip from the cup. 'Is there sugar in this?'

'Yes. Shouldn't there be?' Tara asked, confused.

'It's green tea,' he said. 'It's normally made without sugar.'

Tara flushed. 'I'm sorry,' she said, and reached out to take the cup from him. 'I guess there's a lot I still need to learn. I'll make you another cup.'

Vikram shook his head. 'It's fine,' he said. 'And don't worry about not knowing stuff—I told you, there's a cook and housekeeper who manage the kitchen. You don't need to worry about it. Sit down. I have to go into work for a few hours now, and I need to make sure you don't feel too lost.'

Tara sat down obediently, tucking her legs under the chair, feeling a bit like an underling being briefed on an important project.

'The housekeeper will be coming in at around three—

I asked her to come in a little late today. She takes care of most of the stuff to do with the house, so you don't have to bother about meals or laundry or anything. There are some shops down the road if you need to buy anything. We'll have to share a car right now, but on the weekend I'll see about getting you a car of your own and hiring a second driver. For now, if you need to go somewhere give me a call and I'll send the car back for you.'

Tara wanted to protest that she didn't need a car or a driver, but she was feeling a little out of her depth. The chauffeur-driven luxury car that had come to pick them at the airport had been a bit of a shock, and so had the house—till then, in spite of the diamond ring, the business class travel and luxury honeymoon, it hadn't dawned on her exactly how wealthy her husband was.

Vikram got to his feet, leaving his tea unfinished. 'I'd better change and get ready to leave,' he said, and headed towards the stairs. Halfway there, he came back. 'Not sure how you're doing for money,' he said, and handed her a wad of notes and a debit card. 'Use this for now. I'll figure out getting you a separate bank account in a few days. And a new mobile phone.' He scribbled something on a piece of paper and handed to her along with a set of keys. 'That's the PIN for the card, and here are the house keys.' He gave her a brief smile and headed back towards the stairs.

He was different now, she thought dismally as she watched him run up the stairs two at a time. Ever since they had come back she'd felt like a slightly unwelcome intruder into his busy, ordered life. She looked at the money in her hand—it was at least fifteen thousand.

Three times the amount of money she had ever handled at once.

She wandered around the ground floor of the house. There were two doors leading out of the living room— one led to a small but very well-equipped home gym and the other led to a library. Tara lingered to look at the books, and Vikram found her there when he came downstairs. She was making a face at all the legal tomes that lined one side of the room.

'The fiction section is on the other side,' he said.

'I saw,' she said. 'Not my kind of books.'

She turned around and almost knocked into him. Two warm hands came up to steady her. Her heart was beating a lot faster than normal, and she had to almost physically restrain herself from not leaning into him, losing herself in his arms.

She stepped back, and to defuse the sudden sexual tension touched his tie briefly. 'Cute,' she said, indicating the procession of little grey sheep on a pale yellow silk background.

'Very,' Vikram said, but he wasn't looking at the tie, he was looking right at her, and then he pulled her close for a brief, hard kiss. 'I'll see you in the evening.'

The door shut behind him and Tara gave a little sigh and flopped on to the couch. The smell of his expensive cologne still lingered in the air, and she couldn't help wishing he'd stayed. Weird. At home, she'd always welcomed the rare moments of solitude she got when both her parents were away. She frowned. Marriage shouldn't be changing her in any way. The sex was unexpectedly good, and that was a bonus, but she shouldn't need to keep reminding herself that theirs was a marriage of convenience.

The house felt very empty, Tara realised. Even though she was an only child, she wasn't really used to an empty house—her mother had always been around most of the time. Tara grimaced. She could start unpacking. Or she could call her mother. Or she could go exploring the neighbourhood. The last sounded the most appealing and, slipping the house keys into her pocket, she went out. There was a middle-aged woman in the garden of one of the neighbouring houses, and she smiled cheerfully at Tara as she went past.

Vikram had a crazy few hours at work. His wedding had clashed with the annual leave of the senior partner he worked with, and things had begun to slide horribly while they were both out of office. One of their most important clients was a software company that was entering into a complex multi-country partnership with a Chinese firm, and the deal had run into serious trouble. The team had been working all hours to get things sorted out, but they weren't fully there yet.

Within a few minutes of his reaching his office Vikram was up to his neck in work, switching between client meetings and teleconferences, and trying to catch up on his e-mails in the gaps.

It was past eight-thirty when his secretary popped her head into his office and said reprovingly 'Shouldn't you be going home?'

He was about to snap at her when he realised Tara would be all alone at home, on her first day in a new city.

'Forgotten you were married, hadn't you?' Lillian

chided as he muttered an exclamation and closed his laptop without shutting it down properly.

'No, I'd lost track of time,' he said, and got to his feet. 'Thanks, Lillian. I'd be lost without you. And I'm sorry I kept you back—your kids must be waiting.'

The door didn't open when he tried to turn his key in the lock—it was latched from inside. One of the many things he'd have to get used to, he thought as he rang the bell. Tara opened the door almost immediately. He'd expected her to be upset, or irritated at the delay, but she was neither, giving him a happy little smile as she let him in. She was wearing a long dark-coloured gipsy skirt with a little white T-shirt, and she looked exotic and completely irresistible.

'The cook made a whole lot of stuff she said you like,' she said over her shoulder as she led the way in. 'There's chicken something-or-other, and *rotis* and *biryani,* and all kinds of pickles and *paapads.* I'll lay the table. You must be hungry.'

He was, he realised. He'd skipped lunch, and other than several cups of coffee hadn't had anything since he'd left home. It was nice coming back to a house with someone in it, he thought. Most days the housekeeper had left by the time he came home, and he ended up eating in front of the TV while going over files. Today the table was neatly laid, and Tara was waiting expectantly for him when he got back after freshening up and changing his clothes.

'I should have checked with you—are you OK with meat being cooked in the house?' he asked.

She nodded. 'I'm fine. My friend Ritu's Bengali, and I used to spend loads of time at her place—they cook either fish or chicken every day. And I started eating eggs myself a few years back.' She was touched by his considerateness, however, and even more surprised when he pushed a little box across to her. 'What's this?' she asked, opening it.

This turned out to be a pair of diamond solitaire earrings, and she stared at them for a while in disbelief.

'I ordered them to match the ring, but they weren't delivered in time,' he said. 'My secretary picked them up for me today.'

She didn't look as pleased as he'd expected—actually, she didn't look pleased at all. She looked horrified. He tried to remember if there was anything about diamonds that could potentially upset her. He thought not. He'd been careful to check that there was no plastic in the packaging—that was something she was paranoid about—and to the best of his knowledge diamonds were not part of any kind of fragile ecosystem or anything.

'Don't you like them?' he asked finally, a little irritated by her silence.

She nodded, and turned a troubled face up to him— she looked very young and very confused.

'I do… But you already got me the ring, and your parents gave me heaps of stuff. You didn't need to get me more jewellery.'

He smiled and bent down and kissed her lightly. 'This is a welcome home gift,' he murmured.

'But I haven't got you anything!' she exclaimed.

He laughed. 'You don't need to,' he assured her.

'Actually, I did get you something,' she said shamefacedly. 'Rather, I made it—before we left Jamshedpur. But I didn't give it to you, because, well…'

He was looking at her curiously, and she turned and ran upstairs, coming back in a few minutes with what looked like a bundle of wool.

'It's a scarf,' she said. 'My mum told me I should knit you a sweater, but I'm not that good. It'd have taken me a year to make something your size.'

Vikram shook it out. It was charcoal-grey, a shade he liked, and very neatly and simply made. She must have put hours of effort into it, he thought, feeling absurdly touched.

'This is beautiful,' he said, meaning it, and her face brightened.

'My mum wanted me to put in stripes,' she said. 'But I looked up some designs and copied one I saw on a website for this very posh-sounding British brand. I thought that was the safest.' She dimpled. 'Apparently when my mum was married she made five sweaters for my dad—and two mufflers and dozens of socks. I don't think my dad gave her anything other than her *thaali* and a couple of saris. I'm a complete disgrace to the family, turning up with one measly scarf while you're showering me with diamonds.'

He laughed, but looked at her curiously. 'Are you missing your parents?' he asked. 'I know you wanted to get away to study, but it must be hard being away from them for the first time. And I travel a lot, so you'll be alone often.'

'I think I'll like being alone once in a while,' Tara said. 'I love my parents a lot, but they can be a real pain. My mum's this fountain of guilt. She'll do something really awful, and when I yell at her she'll make me feel so guilty I end up apologising to her. And my dad—well, let's leave that for some other time. He's…complicated.'

'I figured,' Vikram said. 'I guess my parents are a lot easier to deal with. Though they've had a really tough time since my brother died.'

There—he'd said it now. His father had been surprised and sorrowful when he'd found out that he hadn't spoken to Tara about Vijay. But it was a topic he avoided even with people who had known his brother. Tara had stopped eating, and was looking at him sympathetically. Vikram felt he wouldn't be able to bear it if she asked him anything.

'Did you speak to your research guide?' he asked, and thankfully she took the hint and started talking about the work she needed to do for her PhD.

She'd had a full day. She'd met up with one of the other research students who lived nearby, with whom she'd been in touch via e-mail. She'd also picked up some books, and made a friend in a local handicrafts store. She was going to start spending most of the day at the institute from the next week onwards, and Vikram was conscious of a sense of relief. He hadn't been exaggerating when he'd said he travelled a lot, and even when he was in town he worked crazy hours. He'd have hated the thought of Tara sitting alone in an empty house all day while he was away.

Halfway through dinner they had their first argument after the honeymoon.

'I don't need a car,' Tara said. 'A two-wheeler will do.'

Vikram gave her a brief look. 'No,' he said, a little too emphatically

Tara cocked her head to one side. 'Just…*no?*' she asked, wrinkling up her nose. 'People don't just say no to me. They give reasons, and then I argue…'

'Not going to happen here.'

'What if I buy it using my stipend?' Tara asked.

Vikram put his knife and fork down. 'Tara, let's get this straight. You're not using a two-wheeler while you're living with me, and that's final.'

She digested that carefully. 'But is there a reason? Or are you being autocratic just for the fun of it?'

For a second Vikram remembered the weight of Vijay's lifeless body in his arms, and his heart twisted within him so painfully that he could barely breathe. There *was* a reason he didn't want Tara to buy a two-wheeler—a very good reason—but he couldn't bring himself to state it.

'I have certain social standards to maintain in my line of work. I can't have my wife ruining things by careering around on a two-wheeler like a crazy college kid,' he said finally, his voice sounding cold even to his own ears.

'I *was* a college kid till a few months ago,' Tara said quietly. 'And I'm still a student. My family isn't well-off, Vikram. I'm not used to being taken around in a chauffeur-driven car.'

'You'll get used to it soon enough,' Vikram said, getting up and carrying his plate to the sink.

Tara gave him an exasperated look. This particular issue wasn't that important, but she could see life becoming difficult if she gave in to his every whim.

'I'll buy a two-wheeler with my stipend, then, once I get it,' she announced. 'You can—' She stopped mid-sentence as Vikram slammed his plate into the sink and whirled around.

'*No!*' he said. He looked furious, and the veins on his temple were throbbing as he spoke. 'What part of no, you can't have a bike, do you find difficult to understand, Tara?'

No stranger to shouting matches, Tara was about to answer him in kind when she realised that he was almost shaking with rage. There was something going on that she couldn't understand, and puzzlement made her own annoyance abate.

'Why are you getting so upset?' she asked, trying to sound as reasonable as she could. 'It's not such a big deal.'

She watched as Vikram visibly fought for control over himself.

'I'm sorry,' he said briefly, but she could see he didn't mean it. 'I agree it's not such a big deal, so let's just stick with getting you a car, shall we?'

Tara nodded silently, not wanting to push him any further. The tension seemed to leave Vikram's body, but he didn't say anything, merely nodded back and left the room.

For the first time they went to sleep without touching each other. Tara stayed awake for a while. The honeymoon was definitely over, she thought, and it was time she started concentrating on her studies. That was why she was here, after all, she told herself as she turned over and tried to go to sleep. She'd been prepared to make adjustments when she decided to marry him, and she could easily have avoided the fight today.

She drifted off to sleep wishing Vikram had stayed awake for a little while longer so that they could have made up properly. She'd got so used to falling asleep in his arms...

Halfway through the night something woke her up, and she sat up confusedly in bed. Vikram was saying something in his sleep, his mouth working convulsively. The words were so indistinct that she had to lean close to him to understand what he was saying.

It was one phrase, over and over again, and it sounded like, 'No, Vijay. No, no...'

There was an expression of such deep pain and sorrow on his face that it scared her more than it would have if he'd been in the throes of a screaming and thrashing around kind of nightmare. She slid down next to him quickly and put her arms around him, kissing his forehead and trying to pull him closer. He didn't respond, but as she continued to hug him his expression relaxed slowly and he drifted into normal, peaceful slumber. After a while Tara fell asleep as well.

CHAPTER SIX

Return delayed by three days—will be back on sixteenth in time for party. Tara read off her phone screen.

She groaned. The party was on the seventeenth, and she'd been counting on Vikram getting back from China in time to brief her about the guests and tell her what to wear. They'd attended several parties in the three months since they'd been married, and she'd acquired a new wardrobe in consultation with a personal shopper Vikram had hired for her. This one was a bigger affair, though, to be thrown by the senior partners in his firm.

Tara leaned back on the sofa and closed her eyes. Marriage had ended up being so much more and so much less than she'd anticipated. On the surface Vikram was the ideal husband—intelligent, successful, supportive of her career, wonderful in bed. The list went on. Even the slight tinge of arrogance she made so much fun of was attractive. And after that first argument there had been no more fights; he'd been unfailingly charming to her.

She should be over the moon with joy—only, like a greedy pig, she now found that she wanted more from him. He couldn't help the amount he travelled, she knew that, and he made an effort either to e-mail or call each day, wherever he was, and however busy his schedule.

But the e-mails were always polite little three-liners that anyone could have read, and the calls were almost as bad. When he was at home he made a conscious effort to spend as much time with her as she could, but Tara kept getting the feeling he did it because he felt he had to—not because he wanted to.

Only in bed did she feel the barriers between them drop—the sex had grown better with time as she lost a lot of her inhibitions.

On an impulse, she picked the phone up again and dialled Vikram's number. He'd be back in his hotel now, hopefully, and she missed the sound of his voice.

He picked up on the fifth ring, when she was just about to give up and disconnect.

'Tara,' he said. 'Everything OK?'

He sounded preoccupied, and Tara immediately started to feel guilty at having disturbed him.

'Yes,' she replied. 'Sorry—are you busy? I wanted to check a couple of things about the party, but we can speak later—or I'll e-mail you.'

She sounded like a total loser, she thought. Next she'd be making appointments to speak to him through his secretary. Time she went in for some assertiveness.

'We can talk now,' Vikram said. 'The party's our regular annual bash—everyone in the firm and some of our top clients. You know most of the people already.'

Tara made a face. 'Lots of serious conversation about the economy and the stock market, then,' she said. 'And the women will be obsessing about their jewellery and their designer handbags.'

Vikram was silent for a few seconds, and Tara wondered if he was annoyed by the implied criticism. If he was, he didn't show it when he spoke again.

'I guess,' he said. 'You sounded incredibly clued-in the last time, though. As if you'd been hanging around with people like that your entire life.'

'The people I used to hang out with wouldn't know a bear market from a woolly rug,' Tara said. 'I bought a whole bunch of magazines when we came to Bengaluru. Every kind—business, current affairs, society maga-zines—and then I read them from cover to cover and looked up everything I didn't understand on the internet.'

'Effective,' said Vikram. He hadn't realised that she'd put in so much effort, and he felt oddly touched.

Tara laughed. 'It was like a crash course in material-ism. My parents would be proud of me—I'm finally using my studying skills for something practical.'

'Your parents are pretty proud of you already, and with good reason,' Vikram said. 'I know you've had is-sues with your dad, but he's probably your biggest fan.'

'Really?' Tara said disbelievingly. 'He's managed to keep it a pretty closely guarded secret so far, then.'

'He probably didn't want your head turned by idle flattery,' Vikram said.

Tara could visualise him smiling his slow and uncon-sciously sexy smile.

'But he's told me so many times about the grades you've got, and what a support you were to him when your mum was ill.'

Tara felt a little glow of pleasure suffuse her. 'I guess all parents think their kids are the greatest,' she said. 'Whether they admit it or not.'

'Oh, mine never did,' Vikram said lightly. 'They

thought I was self-centred and overly ambitious. Marrying you is probably the only thing I've ever done that they've whole-heartedly approved of.'

'That's not true!' Tara protested. 'Your parents really care about you. It shows every time they look at you. Especially your mum.'

'I guess she can't help it, poor thing. Natural maternal feelings and all that. And besides...' He hesitated a little, and his voice changed, the artificially light-hearted tone growing sombre. 'After Vijay I'm pretty much all they've got. But they don't approve of me, all the same.'

'I'm sure they cared for you just as much before as well,' Tara said. She was now feeling her way through the conversation, and she wished she could see his expression to figure out if she was saying the right thing. 'They must have been disapproving when you were younger and rebelling against them.'

'That's just it. I wasn't rebelling,' Vikram said. 'I genuinely didn't give a hang about what they thought. I went ahead and applied for a law degree without consulting them—not even my dad. And after I left home I didn't visit or call unless I absolutely had to. I was so busy trying to get a winning position in the rat race. Then I started dating a girl they didn't approve of. My mum made an incredible effort to get to know her, and just when they'd begun to understand each other I announced that it was all off.'

He'd paused and, remembering an earlier conversation they'd had, Tara asked, 'Why didn't they approve of Anjali? Because she wasn't from the South?'

Vikram obviously remembered the conversation as well, because he said, 'No, I think I was over-simplifying the issue when I said that. Vijay was seeing a girl who wasn't even Hindu, and my parents loved her from day one. They're not narrow-minded in the least.'

There was a little silence as Tara waited for him to continue.

'Put very crudely, Anjali was high-maintenance,' Vikram said finally. 'She was the youngest in her family, and she'd been petted and spoilt her entire life. She expected a lot from our relationship. My parents knew me well, and they were pretty confident it wouldn't work out.'

'Were you in love with her?' Tara asked.

'I was initially—or at least I thought I was. But after a while the whole thing seemed utterly pointless. Emotional scenes aren't my thing, and I'd be treated to one almost every time we met. To be fair to her, it was far more my fault than hers—I neglected her shamefully—and I was incredibly relieved when she decided to call it quits.'

Tara digested that slowly. She wasn't sure whether he'd told her about Anjali as a warning, or to distract her from the earlier part of the conversation about his parents. Probably the second. With several thousand miles between them he couldn't use sex to lighten things up when the conversation turned too personal.

'Have I succeeded in completely ruining your good opinion of me?' Vikram was asking, his tone casual.

The question seemed serious though, and Tara took heart. 'At least you're honest,' she said. 'That's a quality that will last, hopefully. And I can sympathise with your not liking emotional scenes. They're not my thing, either—though I think a good fight now and then is healthy. Helps to clear the air.'

Vikram began to laugh. 'You're adorable,' he said. 'I suppose you have a little timetable mapped out in your head? Are we overdue for a fight now?'

'Terribly,' she said. 'You've been a big disappointment that way. You're so reasonable and accommodating all the time.'

Vikram shut his eyes for a second. She expected so little from him, he thought. Since they'd come to Bengaluru he'd been travelling almost all the time, and when he was in town he worked crazy hours. By any standards he was a far cry from the perfect husband.

'Send me a list of topics you'd like to fight about and I'll be happy to oblige,' he promised. 'Anything to make my perfectly practical and sensible young wife happy.'

'That makes me sound like something you ordered from a catalogue,' Tara said, sounding deeply disgusted. 'Practical and sensible, indeed. You might as well say I'm house-trained and don't chew the doormats.'

'Rubbish,' Vikram said. 'It's a compliment. If anything, *I'm* the mail-order husband—you picked me out from an ad in the paper, remember?'

'All six foot two inches of you,' Tara agreed. 'Well, if I was doing an appraisal, the way they do in offices, I'd say you've met expectations so far.'

'Not exceeded?' he asked.

She could tell that he was smiling again. 'Noooooo,' she said. 'There's still scope to improve. You could buy me that two-wheeler, for example.'

'Two-wheelers are dangerous,' he said gently. 'I need to ring off now, sweetheart. It's really late here.'

'Goodnight,' Tara said. 'Dream of me tonight.'

'I will,' he said, his voice soft and almost tender.

Tara put the phone down, feeling very mixed-up. Her heart had gone out to Vikram when he was talking about his parents, but she wasn't sure about the Anjali bit. He'd said that he'd been negligent and callous with her, but it didn't sound as if he planned to change his ways. And he'd said that 'practical and sensible' was a compliment. For a few seconds she'd felt quite unreasonably annoyed, and not sensible in the least.

But then he'd called her 'sweetheart', and her defences had melted immediately. He wasn't given to using endearments—not even in bed—so surely it meant something? Or perhaps it had just slipped out unconsciously because he was feeling fond of her for being so 'sensible and practical' as compared to his 'high-maintenance' ex? It was all very confusing, and the feeling that she was slowly but irrevocably falling in love with her husband didn't help.

Sighing, she got up to get her dinner. Marriage was turning out to be a lot more complicated than she'd anticipated.

Vikram got back into Bengaluru only a few hours before the party, with just enough time to get home, shower and change. Tara had got ready early, and was typing away at an article she was writing for a scientific journal. Vikram paused at the door of her study to look at her. She was wearing one of the outfits the personal shopper had chosen for her: a silvery-grey cocktail dress that stopped just short of her knees. Her hair was done up in some kind of complicated pleat, with a few stray strands escaping around her temples, and she looked heartbreakingly lovely. A frown tugged at her forehead as she stopped typing and pored over one of her reference books, chewing her pencil thoughtfully as she read.

Vikram toyed briefly with the idea of taking Tara upstairs, slowly sliding the dress off her, undoing the clips that held up her hair so that it flowed over her naked shoulders… It was an overwhelmingly tempting thought, but he was late already and he couldn't afford to miss the party.

He cleared his throat, and Tara looked around.

'Oh, are we ready to leave?' she asked, getting to her feet and shutting the laptop.

She leaned on him briefly as she slid on her peep-toe heels, and Vikram's resolve almost slipped again. He opened the door and stepped out, taking a few quick breaths of the cold air before Tara joined him and they got into the car.

Vikram's confidence in Tara was justified. She was a hit with everyone at the party.

'Lovely wife you have,' said Justin D'Souza, one of the founding partners of the firm to Vikram in an undertone. 'Manages to get along with women as well as she does with men, and that's not an easy thing for a girl that good-looking.'

Vikram smiled. 'She's quite something,' he said, his eyes following Tara as she moved towards them.

'Done you a deal of good, too, I'd say,' Justin said bluntly. 'You work too hard. You always have. And for the last two years you've practically lived in the office.'

Tara had come up to them, and she caught the last part of the sentence.

Justin beckoned to her. 'You need to get this young man here to take things easy,' he said. 'You're newly-weds. Take a vacation. Enjoy life. Before you know it you'll be old like us and worrying about your kids and your blood pressure.'

Tara laughed, but Justin had made her wonder. All this while she'd thought Vikram worked so hard because he had to, but now it sounded as if he had a choice.

Justin's wife Sharon, a maternal-looking Goan woman in her early forties, began to tell Tara about how her kids were pestering her to get them a pet. 'I'd have agreed, but I know they'll lose interest in the poor unfortunate thing in a week, and it'll starve to death unless I look after it.'

'I had a pet dog when I was a kid,' Tara said. 'I adored her. But she died after she'd been with us only a year. I was heartbroken.'

'Oh, you poor thing!' Sharon said. 'My friend's pug died a few months ago, and she's been so upset her husband is thinking of getting her treated for depression.'

'I can understand a kid being upset,' Justin said. 'But I wonder why adults are affected so badly when a pet dies. I mean, they *know* that animals have shorter lifespans.'

'It's more the case with dogs,' Tara said thoughtfully. 'People tend to treat a dog the way they'd treat a kid— and human emotions are wired to expect a kid to out-live the parents.'

Justin looked impressed 'That's pretty insightful,' he said.

Vikram stood up. 'I don't think the two can compare,' he said shortly. 'Losing a child and losing a dog.'

Tara watched him walk to another set of guests and her heart thudded painfully. She should have known better than to go babbling on about parents losing a kid when she knew his brother had died. And it would be impossible to apologise later. He was so closed off on the subject.

It would never get better, Vikram thought as he mechanically responded to a remark a colleague had addressed to him. A chance comment could make all the blackness and grief of Vijay's death seem as fresh as if it had happened yesterday. Someone mentioning their own brother, an article about a road accident, a photograph of a young man with a smile like Vijay's—all of those had the power to send him spinning back into the black void that his life had become after the accident.

And the guilt… Logically he knew he had no reason to feel guilty, but that didn't change the fact that he did. There was a constant gnawing feeling in the pit of his stomach—a whole squadron of 'ifs' hammering away inside his skull. If not for him his brother wouldn't be dead. His mother wouldn't have that constantly haunted look at the back of her eyes. His father wouldn't go through life like a shell of his former self.

Vikram had had to break the news to his parents—he would never forget the look on his father's face. A cheesy line from an old Hindi movie classic came back to him: 'There is no burden on earth as heavy as the weight of a son's coffin on his father's shoulder.' His dad looked nothing like the wrinkled white-haired actor who played the bereaved father in the movie, and he hadn't broken down and sobbed when he'd learnt of his younger son's death. He had squared his shoulders and put himself to the task of supporting and comforting his wife. But he'd been crushed all the same, greying almost overnight so that he looked a good ten years older than his age.

Tara moved away from the D'Souzas as soon as she could, and went in search of Vikram.

'He's talking to Lisa downstairs,' one of Vikram's assistants volunteered.

'I didn't know Lisa was here,' Tara said. She'd run into Lisa a couple of times since she'd moved to Bengaluru. Once at a party similar to this one, and once accidentally in a store. Both times Lisa had been polite, but not very warm.

'I think she came with Kunal Wilson,' the girl said. 'They're supposed to be dating.'

Tara nodded and headed downstairs. She spotted Vikram and Lisa almost immediately—they were in an alcove near the foot of the stairs, and were standing very close to each other.

'I'd feel so much better if you agreed. I don't even know what you think about the marriage,' Lisa was saying, her voice low and very intense.

Vikram laughed, and the bitterness in the sound made Tara wince. 'I have no rights over you. It doesn't matter what I think.'

'You know it matters,' she replied. 'It matters more than what anyone else thinks—even my own mother.'

'I have nothing against Kunal,' Vikram said. 'I'd probably be equally uncomfortable with the thought of you marrying anyone else, and I'm not going to lie about it to make you feel better.'

'*You* got married,' Lisa said, her voice trembling. 'I don't see you pining away.'

'You have no idea…' Vikram began to say through his teeth. But Lisa was crying now, and Vikram turned quickly and put an arm around her. She clung to him. 'I'm sorry,' he said roughly, and tilted her face up to kiss her on the forehead. 'Don't cry, Lisa.'

He looked up and saw Tara, who was still standing at the foot of the stairs as if rooted to the spot. It had been a very platonic kiss, but seeing another woman in his arms had been a shock to her all the same.

He took a snowy white handkerchief out of his pocket and handed it to Lisa before disengaging himself from her embrace. 'Tara, can you call Kunal, please?' he said, his voice firm and not carrying a trace of the emotion that had filled it a few minutes back.

Tara ran up the stairs and came back with Kunal, who went to Lisa's side and put his arms around her.

Vikram took Tara's arm and walked her up the stairs. 'Sorry you had to see that,' Vikram said briefly. 'Lisa's going through a bit of a bad patch.'

It had sounded more as if Vikram was going through a bad patch, Tara thought silently, but she didn't say anything. She'd never been quite sure of the relationship between Lisa and Vikram—their body language didn't suggest that they had ever been lovers, but there was something very strong between them all the same. Stronger than anything he'd ever felt for *her,* Tara thought, dismayed at how jealous she felt. She'd never seen Vikram display the level of emotion that he had in his altercation with Lisa, and she'd assumed that he wasn't capable of showing strong feelings. Obviously she'd been very wrong.

The party broke up after another hour or so, and Tara

was glad to leave. Her phone rang almost immediately as they got into the car—it was Vikram's mum. A little surprised, because she'd told her earlier in the day that they'd be at the party all evening, she answered the call.

'Have you reached home?' Mrs Krishnan asked.

Tara told her that they were on their way.

'Is Vikram driving?' was her next question.

Tara said, no, the driver was.

'Message me when you reach home, dear,' Mrs Krishnan said.

'But, Amma, it'll take us another half an hour at least, and it's already past twelve. Won't you be asleep?' Tara protested.

'She's calling to check if we're still alive,' Vikram said after she'd put the phone down.

Tara looked over at him, startled by his tone.

'She doesn't sleep if she knows I'm on the road some-where. And now that you're with me she's doubly para-noid. That's why I don't tell her half the time when I'm travelling.'

'Your brother...?' Tara said slowly.

'Died in a bike accident,' Vikram said. 'He called her when he left home to say he'd call her again after class, and—well, he didn't. That's all.'

He sounded almost callous, but his jaw was clenched very tight and Tara didn't know what to say. A conven-tional sympathetic response would be woefully inad-equate, and he didn't look as if he'd appreciate being touched right now. She stayed silent till they reached home, feeling very troubled.

'I have to leave for the airport early tomorrow, Satish,' Vikram told the driver. 'You'll need to be here at five.'

She'd forgotten he was off again the next day. Tara glanced at her watch. It was late, and probably not the best time to start a serious discussion, but it couldn't be helped.

'Why was Lisa upset?' she asked quietly once they were inside the house.

Vikram shrugged. 'Something to do with marrying Kunal. Do you need anything from outside, or should I lock up?'

'You can lock up,' Tara said. 'Why was she sobbing all over you, then?' It came out sounding a little ruder than she'd intended, as if Lisa was a hysterical man-eater, and that wasn't what she'd meant to imply. 'I mean, I couldn't help hearing part of what she said, and it sounded like she wanted your blessing on the marriage, or something of that sort.'

'Something of that sort,' Vikram agreed, his voice bland.

Tara gave him a long look. 'If you think it's none of my business you can say so, and I'll shut up,' she said. 'This is turning into a session of *Twenty Questions*.'

Vikram passed a hand over his face. He looked tired, Tara thought, a quick pang of guilt shooting through her. He was probably still jet-lagged, and it was late, and he had to travel again the next day. What was she thinking, shooting questions at him like a police interrogator?

'Lisa was engaged to Vijay,' Vikram said finally. 'Does that help explain matters?'

He wasn't being sarcastic, but Tara felt her face heat up. God, she should have guessed it when she'd heard Vikram telling Lisa that he'd be uncomfortable with the thought of her marrying anyone, not just Kunal. And he'd also told her earlier that Vijay's girlfriend hadn't been Hindu. Lisa was a Christian, and she was very close to Vikram's family. It was so obvious that only an utter dimwit would have missed it.

'I'm sorry,' she said miserably, not sure what she was apologising for. Not guessing, suspecting Vikram of having something going on with Lisa, or for her general lack of sensitivity and good sense. As usual her guilt glands had gone into overdrive, and she was beginning to feel single-handedly responsible for the evening's debacle.

Vikram didn't give any sign of having heard her as he moved around the hallway, putting his shoes into the shoe rack and fiddling with the complicated system of locks that they'd installed after a recent theft in the neighbourhood. He wasn't looking at her, and after hesitating at the foot of the stairs for a few minutes Tara quietly went up to their bedroom.

She was putting her jewellery away in the safe when Vikram came upstairs. 'Do you need help packing?' she asked over her shoulder by way of further apology—he normally did his packing himself.

He didn't say anything, but came up behind her and, putting his arms around her, buried his face in her shoulder. She stood very still. He held her for a while, very tight, neither of them saying anything, and then he turned her around and sought her mouth with a kind of blind desperation.

They barely made it to the bed, and their lovemaking was wilder and more passionate than it had ever been before. For the first time since she'd married him Tara felt that Vikram actually needed her—needed her in a visceral way that had nothing to do with sex. It wasn't a happy feeling, though—it was tied in too closely with the feeling that they didn't really understand or connect with each other yet.

CHAPTER SEVEN

VIKRAM was gone by the time Tara woke up, and she decided to stay in bed a little longer and enjoy a lie-in. She didn't have to go to the institute—there was a paper she needed to type up, but that could wait.

She was reliving the previous night in her mind when the doorbell rang.

Tara dragged herself out of bed and went to open the door. Lisa was standing on the doorstep, a tentative smile on her lips. Still half-asleep, Tara gaped at her, and stupidly said the first thing that came into her head. 'Vikram isn't home.'

'No, I know he isn't,' Lisa said. 'I came to see you, actually. Is this a bad time? I should have called, but I was passing by and decided to take a chance.'

'That's fine. Come on in,' Tara said, wishing she'd got up on time. Her hair was a mess, half in its braid and half out, and she hadn't even brushed her teeth yet. Lisa was, as usual, perfectly turned out in a pink linen shirt and white Capri pants. Tara ushered her into the living room, and ran upstairs to freshen up.

'I'm sorry about the scene yesterday,' Lisa said when Tara re-entered the room. 'I'm sure Vikram explained, but I wanted to apologise in person.'

Tara hesitated. It felt odd confessing to someone who was almost a stranger that her husband kept her in a state of perpetual cluelessness as far as his life was concerned. Only if Lisa was about to launch into a long explanation—which she seemed set on doing—it made sense to be upfront. 'Vikram didn't say much, actually.'

Lisa looked upset. 'You must think I'm absolutely nuts, then!' she said. 'You know about me and Vijay, of course?'

Tara nodded.

'I met him here—in this room, actually,' Lisa said. 'He had just moved here to do an MBA course when Vikram hired me to do up his house.' She smiled briefly, her mind obviously elsewhere. 'It was the first project I was handling completely on my own—I'd only been helping my mum till then. And then, of course, I had to fall head over heels for my client's little brother. We dated for some months, and then he asked me to marry him. He still had one semester to go before he completed his MBA, but he had several job offers in hand already, and he said he wanted to get married as soon as he graduated. And then, of course…'

Lisa's voice trailed off, and Tara stayed silent as well.

'It's been three years now, and I still can't talk about it without breaking down,' Lisa said finally. 'It was such a shock. He'd pestered Vikram to buy him a motorcycle for his birthday. He was riding it to college without a helmet when a truck hit him.'

Tara winced. Vikram had mentioned a bike accident, but not the details. It wasn't surprising he'd refused to buy her a two-wheeler—though he'd lied about the reason.

Lisa said, 'I've known Kunal for a while now, and a

month ago he asked me to marry him. I still love Vijay, but I love Kunal, too. It's different with Kunal. I don't feel I'm being disloyal to Vijay—I won't forget him ever.'

'But Vikram doesn't see it that way?' Tara asked. It was an unreasonable attitude from her point of view—Lisa couldn't be expected to mourn Vijay for the rest of her life.

'He was OK with my marrying in theory. He actually said he thought it a good idea.'

Tara frowned—he hadn't sounded OK the night before.

'I think I was pushing my luck,' Lisa said. 'You see, if I'd married Vijay we'd probably have had a Hindu wedding, but Kunal's Catholic, like me, and we're getting married in church. My dad isn't alive any more, and I don't have a brother. I wanted Vikram to give me away at the wedding and he said no.'

That was understandable, Tara thought. Asking him to participate actively in the ceremony was not very fair.

Evidently Lisa had come around to that point of view as well. 'I'm not going to pester him about it any more,' she said. 'It's OK even if he decides to skip the wedding.' Her voice faltered a little. 'Though I really, really want both of you to be there.' She took Tara's hand between hers and pressed it gently. 'I'm so happy Vikram married you. You're just what he needs.'

Tara looked a little surprised. 'You're calm and sensible, and even though you're so young you're a lot more mature than people twice your age.'

There was that word *sensible* again, but it didn't sound so bad when someone was telling her that she was just what Vikram needed.

Tara grinned and asked, 'Why do I get this feeling you're comparing me to someone?'

Lisa laughed. 'I am, actually. Poor Anjali. She was clingy and insecure, and she didn't know how to handle Vikram at all.' She got to her feet in one fluid movement. 'I need to rush. I'm running late for a meeting.' She hugged Tara impulsively. 'Let's catch up properly some time—just the two of us, a girls' night out. And, thanks—you've been an absolute sweetheart. Vikram's a lucky guy.'

Not objecting to her husband being cried over in public was evidently a big plus point in her favour, Tara thought wryly as she shut the door behind Lisa. As was being calm and sensible. She felt anything but calm and sensible now—she'd found out a lot about her husband in the last fifteen minutes and she wished he'd been more open with her.

After Lisa left Tara felt way too restless to work on her report. She'd given the housekeeper a day off, and for a while she puttered around the house, rearranging the spice jars on the kitchen shelves and making a list of groceries that needed to be ordered. Halfway through scrubbing out the refrigerator she threw her mop down in exasperation.

'I'm turning into my mum,' she muttered, standing up and slamming the refrigerator door shut. 'I have a day to myself, and all I can think of doing is cleaning.'

She went upstairs and changed into jeans and a long-sleeved T-shirt, shaking her abundant hair out of its plait to comb it. She looked at her reflection in dissatisfaction. There was still something very schoolgirlish about her face, she thought. *'You're so young,'* Lisa's voice came back to her. Time to do something about it.

'Are you sure you want to cut it?' the stylist in the neighbourhood beauty salon asked ten minutes later, weighing her hair in one hand and looking at her quizzically in the mirror. 'It'll take years to grow it to this length again.'

'I'm not planning to grow it again,' Tara said briefly. A little pang went through her as she remembered Vikram running his fingers through her hair, wrapping it round his hand and tugging gently to bring her closer to him. She dispelled the image firmly. Vikram didn't have to spend hours every week shampooing and conditioning and drying—and, anyway, what did it matter what *he* thought?

An hour later her hair reached just below her shoulders, curling into natural ringlets at the ends. It still felt a little odd—she was so used to the weight—but she felt lighter and freer somehow. And there was no doubt it looked fabulous. Even the stylist looked impressed as he tweaked the last few curls into place.

'You're lucky,' he said. 'This style suits you a lot better than long hair did.'

'I told you, didn't I?' Tara said with a cheeky little grin as she pressed a tip into his hand. 'You wanted me to go around looking like Rapunzel for the rest of my life.'

The man grinned back, pocketing the tip and wishing all his customers were as pretty and as easy to please.

Vikram came back two weeks later, having firmly resolved not to travel any more for the next few months. He told himself that it was because he needed to concentrate on things in office for a while, and because it wasn't fair to Tara, leaving her alone for such long stretches of time. He'd even been away during the Tamil New Year. The first New Year after a wedding was supposed to be a big deal, and his mother was still grousing about his not having been around.

He owed it to Tara to hang around for a while, he told himself. But the truth was he couldn't wait to get back to his wife. He'd even started dreaming about her, and reaching out for her in the middle of the night before waking with a start when he realised the bed was empty. It was just the sex that he missed, he told himself. And, of course, she was an engaging companion—sharp-witted, with a keen sense of the ridiculous. That was it, he told himself firmly. He'd made a pact with himself some years ago, after he'd split up with Anjali, that he'd never con himself into believing that he loved a woman again. He wasn't capable of managing a relationship that involved the word *love,* and no one deserved having their life messed up because of him, specially not Tara.

He'd taken an early afternoon flight, and the house was empty when he got there. The housekeeper had left, and Tara was still at the institute. He contemplated calling her and suggesting he pick her up and take her out for dinner, but that smacked a little of desperation. Instead he pulled out some files that were long overdue for attention and got down to work.

It was almost dark when the door clicked open and Tara came in, carrying her laptop and a bag of books, her hair swinging jauntily around her shoulders.

Vikram stared at her for a while, his expression blank. 'You've cut your hair,' he said finally.

Tara looked at him uncertainly. He looked shaken, as if she'd grown a moustache or dyed her eyebrows purple instead of having had a simple haircut.

'This is a lot more convenient,' she said. 'All that hair used to give me headaches, but my parents never let me trim it.'

'Right,' he said, but he couldn't stop himself staring. Her long, waist-length hair had been one of the things he'd found most attractive about Tara. Of course she was still the same person with her hair shorter, but he felt an absurd sense of loss. 'You didn't tell me you were going to cut it,' he said without thinking. 'I loved your hair.'

'You didn't tell me when *you* got a haircut,' she retorted. He had used the word 'loved' for her *hair,* of all things! That stung—especially since he'd said it unconsciously. 'Maybe next time I'll send you an e-mail, asking for your permission.'

Vikram shook himself. 'Sorry,' he said, raising his hands in a gesture of surrender. 'You're right. I've no business complaining. How've you been? Did you miss me?'

'Terribly,' Tara said, keeping her voice light. It wouldn't do to let him see quite how much. 'Especially the sound of your phone pinging every ten seconds.'

He raised his eyebrows. 'Are you trying to tell me something?'

'Maybe I am.' She turned away and began fiddling with her bag. 'I hardly get to see you, do I? Even when you're in town.'

It was the first time she'd even come close to complaining, and Vikram found that instead of feeling annoyed he felt a fierce and unexpected sense of pleasure.

'I mean, I know what your work's like,' she added quickly. 'It'd be nice to see you around more, that's all.' Vikram was looking at her almost tenderly, and she felt her heartbeat quicken.

It was on the tip of his tongue to tell her that he'd decided to cut down on travelling, but he held back. 'You'd probably get tired of me if I was in town all the time,' he said instead, deciding to see how things went before he committed to something that might end up worsening things between them in the long run.

Tara shrugged. 'Perhaps. We might run out of things to say to each other.' She felt terribly let down. For a second she'd actually thought he was going to admit to being more than casually fond of her. Evidently not. She caught his eyes wandering towards her hair again, and rapped out angrily, 'Stop. Staring. At. My. Hair.'

Vikram laughed. 'I'm trying to get used to it. Come here.' He held a hand out to her and she came unwillingly.

'Everyone else says it looks good,' she muttered as he pulled her close. 'Not that they'd have to "get used to it".'

'Everyone else isn't married to you,' Vikram said, nuzzling her neck. 'Who's everyone else, anyway? I thought you'd been buried away in the institute?'

'There are other human beings there, you know,' Tara said, breaking away from him. She still felt annoyed, and a little tearful, and she didn't want to get close to him until she'd regained control over herself.

'Ah, really?' Vikram said, teasing her now, his lips twitching slightly. 'Like the sixty-year-old professors you told me about?'

'Not all of them are sixty,' Tara said. 'And it's the other research students I hang out with, not the professors.'

Vikram frowned. It was logical, really, that there'd be other students her age, but most of Tara's conversation about the institute was centred around the near-mythical figure of Dr Shanta, her research supervisor. He hadn't really thought of her having friends there.

'Why don't you invite them over some time?' he asked. 'These guys you hang around with?'

'Not posh enough for you,' Tara said briefly. 'You'd find them nerdy and boring, and they'd be scared stiff of you.'

'I'm sure I wouldn't,' Vikram protested. She was making him out to be some kind of control freak snob. 'If they're your friends I'll get along with them fine. Go on—invite them over.'

'They're just guys I work with,' Tara muttered. She thought of Ritu. 'My real friends are back home. But if you really want to meet this bunch, Dr Shanta's invited us over to her Holi party this Saturday. I said no, because I didn't think you'd be interested.' She looked up just in time to catch the appalled expression on his face and began to laugh. 'Oh, dear. Obviously Holi parties aren't your thing. Let's just leave it, shall we?'

'No, we'll go,' Vikram said. She was right—he hated the festival. But he didn't want to back down now. Noise, people rubbing colour into each other's faces, kids running around with water guns... It was his idea of a first-class nightmare.

'You don't have to,' Tara said, coming closer to him and putting both hands on his chest, sliding them up slowly to meet at the back of his neck. 'I'll even admit you're not as much of a snob as you look.' She stood on tiptoe slightly, reaching up to touch her lips to his and run her tongue seductively along his lower lip.

'We'll go,' Vikram said and, picking her up bodily, carried her across to the nearest flat surface—which happened to be a sofa. Carefully, he deposited her there, and started removing her clothes one by one as she struggled and laughed. Then, when every stitch of clothing was gone, he covered her body with his, absorbing her moans into his very skin.

At the back of his mind nagged the thought that perhaps, already, he was allowing himself to care too much.

CHAPTER EIGHT

SATURDAY morning dawned bright and sunny, but Vikram groaned as he got out of bed.

'We can still cancel,' Tara called out from the bathroom.

He shook his head. He had another reason for wanting to go now. Ever since he'd come back he could feel his reactions to Tara going out of control, and he badly needed to put some distance between them. He couldn't think of a better way to do that than to attend a noisy, rowdy party thrown by a bunch of post-grad students he'd never met before.

'You brought colours?' Vikram asked later, raising his eyebrows as Tara slid into the car's passenger seat next to him.

'It's a Holi party,' Tara said patiently. 'You're expected to bring colours. Besides, these are organic. Dr Shanta said she'd throw out anyone who gets chemical colours.' She rummaged in the eco-friendly cloth bag at her feet. 'I even got a water gun. Recycled plastic.'

Vikram groaned again, throwing the car into gear and moving forward.

Tara was looking critically out of the window. 'Holi isn't such a big thing in this part of the country, is it?'

'Not really,' Vikram said, concentrating on the road. 'It's more of a North Indian thing. I haven't played it in years—though Anjali did try to drag me into something last year.'

'You didn't go?'

'I couldn't. Lisa was going through a tough time and I had to be with her.'

Tara gave him a quick look. No wonder Anjali had been 'clingy and insecure' as Lisa had described her—being Vikram's girlfriend while he rushed around playing nursemaid to another woman had to have been tough. He was looking rather grim now, but she risked another question. 'Did they get along? Anjali and Lisa, I mean?'

Vikram shook his head. 'Anjali didn't like Lisa taking up so much of my time—she even accused Lisa of wanting me for herself.' His jaw tightened slightly. 'There was quite a scene.'

How surprising, Tara felt like saying, but she kept her lips carefully buttoned together. Knowing Vikram, she could imagine him not having bothered to explain why Lisa was so emotionally dependent on him. Poor Anjali, she thought, feeling quite indignant on her behalf.

'Say it,' Vikram advised, sounding amused. 'I can tell you're bottling up some perfectly scathing comments.'

Tara flushed. 'I was just thinking that you and Lisa are rather hard on Anjali, that's all.'

Vikram took his eyes off the road to look at her, and all traces of amusement had left his voice when he said, 'When has Lisa discussed Anjali with you?'

Oops. She hadn't told Vikram about Lisa's visit, thinking that it might worsen the situation between the two of them. Now he sounded positively furious.

'She came by the house once when you were away. It was the day after the party. She wanted to apologise for creating a scene. And we've talked on the phone a few times. She only mentioned Anjali once.'

Vikram's lips thinned. 'I'm sure she said enough that once.'

'She only said that Anjali was a little insecure,' Tara said, wishing she hadn't brought Lisa into the conversation. 'She wasn't criticising her, or anything. It was a passing comment.'

'If Anjali was insecure, it was far more my fault than hers,' Vikram said tightly. 'I should have told her right up front that the kind of true love she was looking for wasn't something I believed in.'

'As in you don't believe it exists? Or you don't believe it'd have worked for you?'

'Both.' There was a little pause as he navigated a busy crossing. Then he said, 'I don't think the kind of love they talk about in romance novels and Bollywood movies is something I'm capable of. And people who claim to be in love are often deluding themselves. Look at Lisa— if Vijay really was the love of her life, she wouldn't be marrying Kunal now.'

Tempted to jump to Lisa's defence, Tara held back. Presumably Lisa could take care of herself, but Vikram's saying he didn't believe in love was deeply disturbing. It was something she'd said herself in the past but, looking back, she realised she hadn't really meant it. She'd been going by what she'd seen of her parents' marriage, and had assumed that love had no place in a practical world. Her views had changed a lot since then—she was only a few steps away from falling in love with Vikram herself, and the only thing holding her back was his coldness.

'And so you settled for an arranged marriage?' she said, just to make sure.

'Yes,' he replied.

Tara clenched her hands in her lap. So that was that, then. And he'd been upfront about it from the day they'd met. She only had herself to blame for the nasty cold feeling that was settling around her heart.

It was ten-thirty by the time they reached the students' hall where the party was being held. A couple of vaguely familiar-looking young men came up to Vikram, one of them leaning up respectfully to put a *tikka* on his forehead and a small smear of colour on his cheek. Tara had disappeared into the hall, and for a second Vikram felt a few decades older than his real age as he contrasted the polite smiles of the boys next to him with the utter pandemonium inside.

Then he caught sight of fifty-year-old Dr Shanta, pelting one of her students with water-filled balloons, her grey hair streaming out behind her. When in a Holi party... He grabbed the young man nearest him and, taking a packet of powdered colour, liberally smeared a fistful on his cheeks.

'Happy Holi,' he said to the flabbergasted boy, and strode into the hall to find his vanished wife.

Tara was being chased by a bunch of girls whom she'd unwisely attacked first with her water gun. 'Help!' she squealed, flinging herself into Vikram's arms.

He laughed, shielding her with his body as someone threw an entire bucket of coloured water at them.

Tara emerged from the dunking, shaking her hair and

wringing the water out of the hem of her *kurta*. 'Just you wait,' she called out at the giggling girls, grabbing a few packets of colour from a nearby table and running after them.

'Such a vibrant, enthusiastic girl,' Dr Shanta said affectionately as she came to stand next to Vikram. 'She's one of my favourite students.'

Vikram turned to smile at his wife's research supervisor. 'She's very grateful for all the help you gave her when she applied for her PhD.'

Dr Shanta waved her hand impatiently. 'Help—shelp,' she said. 'The girl is brilliant. And her stupid parents were doing everything they could to hold her back.' She glowered into the distance for a few seconds, and several students who caught her eye by mistake melted away. 'Some people don't deserve to have bright children. I was so glad when she called and told me she was marrying you. I wanted her to have time free for her research, not be slaving away at a part-time job to make ends meet.' She fixed Vikram with a firm eye. 'I hope you're not treating her career as some kind of hobby that'll keep her busy until you decide to have children?'

Normally Vikram would have resented the question, but it was difficult to resent anything Dr Shanta said. She so obviously had Tara's interests at heart.

'I don't understand the field too well,' he said honestly. 'But I don't regard Tara's career as a hobby. It's such an integral part of who she is.' He smiled briefly. 'I don't think she'd have married me if it weren't for her wanting to come here and work with you. As for children—it's not something we've discussed yet. I'm in no hurry—I'm not sure I even want children.'

Dr Shanta gave him a sharp look. 'Tara wants kids, from what I understand, so you'll end up having them. It's not like you men have to do any of the work anyway. I understand wanting to have children. I have children of my own. It's just that so many of my brightest female students are now housewives because they felt they couldn't manage a family *and* stay committed to research work. I'd be very disappointed if Tara went that way.'

'I'm sure she won't,' Vikram said abruptly.

He hadn't known Tara wanted kids, and he felt a little aggrieved at her discussing the topic with Dr Shanta without ever having mentioned it to him. Then his sense of fairness reasserted itself. It was likely she'd just been answering one of Dr Shanta's pointed questions. She probably wanted kids some time in the future—most women did. She was way too young to be thinking of them now. One of the reasons he'd wanted to marry a younger woman rather than someone near his own age was because she'd be in no hurry to have a family.

Kids. He knew one of the reasons his mother had wanted him to marry was because she desperately wanted grandchildren. A mirthless smile crossed his face. Dr Shanta didn't need to worry about Tara neglecting her research because she had to manage kids—they had a ready-made baby-minder in his mum.

He was confident of controlling his feelings towards Tara, but kids were something else altogether. You couldn't stop yourself from loving a child, and he wasn't sure when he would be ready for that kind of emotional complication. Very briefly his mind flashed back to the day his parents had brought Vijay back from the hospital. He'd been seven, and his mother had been worried about how he'd react to having a sibling after being an only child for so long.

The baby had seemed so tiny, wrapped up in a little shawl, his little hands balled into fists. He'd been fast asleep, not opening his eyes even when their mother had put him gently into Vikram's arms. Vikram remembered the sharp current of love and protectiveness that had run through him—he'd resisted when his mother tried to take the baby back.

Vikram looked blindly at the group of students still happily chasing each other around. His brother and he had been unusually close, in spite of the age difference. Oh, they'd fought, and at times Vijay had deeply resented his big brother bossing him around, but he'd missed him terribly when Vikram had moved out of home. And even several years later, when he had a choice of cities in which to do his MBA, he'd given up a better institute in Ahmedabad and come to Bengaluru so that he could be near his brother.

Their parents had counted on Vikram to look after Vijay—and he had, after a fashion, taking him around the city on weekends, buying him a new mobile phone and an iPod. The motorcycle was something he and his parents had argued about a lot. Vijay had desperately wanted a bike, and his parents had thought it unsafe. Vikram had thought their parents were being unnecessarily paranoid and had bought him one on his birthday— Vijay had been ecstatic. A month later he was dead. Their parents' fears had been realised in the most tragic way. They hadn't reproached him even once, but the guilt ate away at Vikram anyway.

Tara realised after a while that Vikram was standing

to the side, not playing Holi any longer. She stopped to look at him worriedly, but Dr Shanta gave her a little push.

'Your husband can take care of himself,' she said. 'In any case, I'm going to call a stop to this after another five minutes. I'm too old to run around any more. Anyone who still wants to play will have to go back to the hostels. Otherwise there's beer and biryani at my place in half an hour, after everyone's cleaned up.'

Most of the students were running out of organic, non-toxic colours, and were more than willing to stop.

Vikram didn't notice until Tara came up to him. She was wringing wet, her originally pink *salwar kameez* was now every colour of the rainbow, and her face had so much colour on it he could hardly recognise her.

'I'm going to the women's hostel to shower and change,' she said. 'We'll be having lunch in half an hour. You can go with Deepak or Varun to the men's hostel and clean up, if you like.' She took in his unusually still expression, and asked, 'Is everything OK?'

'Yes, of course,' Vikram said curtly. 'I'll see you in a bit, then.'

When Tara rejoined him twenty minutes later he was holding a mug of beer and listening to a heated discussion on cricket. She went up to him and slipped her hand into his arm. 'Did you get very bored?' she asked in an undertone.

Vikram shook his head, feeling a little guilty about his earlier brusqueness.

'Not at all.' He reached out and tucked a strand of hair behind her ear. 'You haven't got all the colour off,' he said. 'There're streaks of pink down your neck.'

He caressed her neck gently with the backs of his fingers and she felt a rosy flush suffuse her cheeks. Even after several months of marriage his touch had the power to make her forget everything else. 'I'll—I'll scrub it off properly once we get home,' she stammered.

Vikram took pity on her and removed his hand. 'I'm going to grab some lunch,' he said. 'Join me on the lawn once you're ready.'

Tara heaped her plate with vegetable biryani and plonked herself on the lawn next to him five minutes later.

'Beer?' Vikram asked, and she shook her head.

'I hate the taste,' she said. 'I tried it a couple of times at your office parties, remember?'

He didn't—though he did remember her trying vodka once and grimacing at the taste.

'Isn't *bhaang* the official Holi drink?' he asked.

'I did suggest serving it,' said Dr Shanta's husband, Professor Dubey, overhearing and stopping next to them. 'But Shanta thought it would set a bad example, and the next thing we knew we'd have students coming to classes doped out of their minds.'

'Which a lot of them do in any case,' Tara said in an undertone, once Professor Dubey moved to the next group of students. 'I guess serving *bhang* would make it official.'

Vikram laughed. 'Dr Shanta's quite the mother hen, isn't she?' he asked. 'In spite of the tough exterior. It's interesting to see how you fit in so well with these people, even though you've known them only for a few months.'

'They're like family now,' Tara said, and then, realising how it sounded, 'I mean...'

'I know what you mean,' Vikram said. 'I'm not around much, am I? And my friends aren't your type.'

'It's not that…' Tara fumbled. But he was right, and they both knew it.

Tara had done a superb job of adjusting to Vikram's social circle, but given a choice she far preferred hanging out with her research colleagues, wearing old clothes and arguing about things like cricket and global warming and the Loch Ness monster. No designer dresses, no branded handbags, no long and pointless discussions about the economy and the stock market.

With a slight shock Vikram realised how little effort he'd made to get to know her friends, or even her likes and dislikes. Almost any person selected at random from the gathering around them probably knew the real Tara better than he did. Almost any person selected at random also had probably spent more waking hours with her than he had.

His guilt only deepened when Tara asked worriedly, 'Did Dr Shanta say something you didn't like? I saw you frowning after she went away—she can be really blunt sometimes.'

Vikram shook his head, and then, 'Something she said reminded me of Vijay,' he said. He saw Tara tense up immediately.

'I'm sorry—' she started to say, but Vikram put a hand over hers for a brief second.

'Don't be,' he said. 'I've no idea why I reacted so strongly. It seems to be getting worse with time, not better. For the first couple of years after Vijay died I managed fine—at least in public—but now I can't stop thinking about him.'

There was a brief pause. Vikram had ended up say-ing more than he'd intended, and had begun to regret it.

Tara was silent as she turned over Vikram's last state-ment in her head. 'But you can't help it, right?' she asked. 'You can't force yourself to stop thinking about Vijay, and you shouldn't. It isn't natural, not thinking about him. And there aren't any time limits to grief, are there?' She flushed as Vikram turned to look at her. 'Sorry. I'll shut up. It's not like I know anything about it.'

'I think I said this to you the day we met—you apolo-gise too often,' Vikram said. 'None of this is your fault.'

Of course it wasn't, Tara thought, but sometimes Vikram behaved as if it was his. It sounded as if he didn't feel he had the right to grieve for his brother, and that was just plain wrong. Unwilling to let the topic slide, she asked, 'What was Vijay like?'

Vikram smiled unexpectedly. 'You'd have liked him,' he said. 'He was so full of life. There were always a hun-dred things he'd be trying to do at once. He looked quite a lot like me, but he was shorter and thinner—he used to say we were Dr Jekyll and Mr Hyde versions of each other. He insisted that he was Dr Jekyll, of course. And he had the most amazing amount of cheek—could get away with pretty much anything. Big loss to the crime world, him being born into a respectable law-abiding family, we always told him.'

'And with a lawyer brother to boot,' Tara said.

'Oh, he hated the idea of me being a lawyer almost as much as my parents did,' Vikram said. 'But he was coming round to it. And he had this little notebook of business ideas he kept jotting down and doing nothing about—he planned to sell the ideas one by one, and he was counting on me protecting his intellectual property rights for him.'

'What kind of ideas?' Tara asked, genuinely curious and hoping no one would come and interrupt them.

'All kinds. Some of them were really crazy—like a mobile phone application he'd designed for jealous wives to track their husband's doings. You loaded it onto the husband's phone in secret, and it sent his location and a copy of all text messages he sent to the wife's phone. He put in around six months of efforts designing the thing, tested it on my phone and my dad's, and then suddenly decided it wasn't "ethically right" and destroyed all the files. And there was an Impress the Chicks training course for nerds.'

Tara opened her mouth to ask a question and Vikram shook his head.

'Don't ask. It was too complicated for me to get my head around. Whatever it was, it must have worked for him—he had Lisa wrapped around his little finger in a couple of days.' Vikram fell silent for a few seconds. 'So, yeah,' he said finally. 'He was a good kid. And he kind of held our family together—my parents are lost without him. I've lived away from them for so long that I don't really connect with them any more. And, as I told you, I never was the ideal son.'

'But your parents are really proud of you,' Tara said, not liking his implication.

'Yes, I know that,' Vikram replied. 'I've done pretty well as far as material things go.' He looked away. 'It's the important stuff that I've screwed up on.'

Tara didn't know what to say, but a second later he was speaking again.

'We should join the others,' he said, standing up and reaching out a hand to help Tara up.

She stood, her brow creased in worry. 'I wish...' she started to say.

He interrupted her. 'That you could do something? I know.' He gave a mirthless smile. 'Don't waste your energy feeling sorry for me. I could have prevented Vijay dying and I didn't. I need to learn to live with that.'

'The accident wasn't your fault!' Tara exclaimed.

'I got him the bike,' Vikram replied. 'My parents told me not to, but I went ahead and did it anyway because I thought I knew better. He didn't wear a helmet most of the time, and I didn't say anything. Nothing he took seriously at least. I was seven years older than him, Tara. It was my job to look after him.'

He turned away and began to stride across the lawn. Tara gave a helpless little shrug and followed him. She badly wanted to contradict him, to explain that he wasn't being logical, but she could hardly do it in front of a dozen fellow students. Her heart twisting, she went to stand beside Vikram as he replied politely to a remark Prof Dubey addressed to him.

CHAPTER NINE

'Do you mind if I drop you home and go out for a bit?'
Vikram asked as they got into the car fifteen minutes
later. 'I need to meet someone.'

'Sure,' Tara said, trying not to show her disappointment.

She'd been unconsciously looking forward to spending
the rest of the day with Vikram. Since the honeymoon
they hadn't had much time alone together, except in bed.
Vikram was always travelling, or working even on the
weekends, and a whirl of social engagements filled up
whatever little spare time he had. Being married to him
was a lot like being a celebrity wife, she thought wryly,
except that she didn't get her face in the papers.

Vikram put the car into gear and reversed out of the
parking lot. He hadn't missed the downcast look on Tara's
face but he hardened his heart against it. The meeting
he had wasn't urgent. It was with an old schoolfriend
who'd been badgering him for free advice on a property
dispute and he could have called it off easily—he didn't
even like the man much.

Taking Tara home and spending the afternoon in bed
with her was an amazingly tempting thought. If he shut
his eyes for a second he'd be able to imagine her silken

limbs twining around him, her soft moans in his ears. He mentally shook himself to dispel the image, remembering instead the telltale sympathy he'd seen in her eyes when he'd spoken about Vijay. Irrationally, he felt angry with her—almost as if she'd tricked him into revealing more of his feelings to her than he'd intended. It wasn't her fault—he knew that—but the afternoon's conversation seemed to have further compromised the simple, almost transactional relationship he'd had with her, and he badly wanted some temporary distance between them.

'I'll be back by five,' he offered as a kind of sop. 'If you like we can start with your driving lessons today.' He'd offered to teach her to drive soon after they got married, but so far hadn't been able to spare the time.

'I enrolled in classes a month ago,' Tara said. 'I should get my licence in a couple of weeks.'

Vikram didn't reply immediately, but as Tara glanced at him she saw a slight frown crease his forehead. Maybe he'd expected her to tell him, but the topic hadn't come up. And, honestly, he couldn't expect her to go into voluntary cold storage while he was away.

Her little flare of annoyance subsided as she remembered the expression on his face when he'd said he was responsible for Vijay's death. She'd ached to put her arms around him and tell him to stop torturing himself, only she'd known it wouldn't be any use.

'So, can you drive now?' Vikram asked, breaking into her thoughts.

'Kind of,' she said cautiously. 'I know how to change gears and reverse. And I park pretty well.' She hated driving from the bottom of her heart—but she wasn't about to tell him that.

'Let's get you some driving practice in the evening, then,' he said. 'We can drive down the airport road and back, and go out for dinner afterwards.'

'Sure,' Tara said unenthusiastically.

He laughed, reaching out and trailing the back of his hand gently down her cheek. Tara had a second's impulse to take his hand and press her lips to it. She suppressed it ruthlessly. Vikram didn't handle sentimental gestures very well—he'd freeze up and retreat into his shell.

'Keep your hands on the wheel,' she said instead, tapping his hand smartly as it wandered lower. 'We'll land up in a ditch.'

He laughed and removed his hand. 'I think your phone is ringing,' he remarked.

'Damn, so it is,' Tara said, grabbing her bag and digging frantically in it. She'd been so engrossed in managing her reactions to Vikram she hadn't heard it ring.

'What on earth do you keep in that bag?' Vikram asked. 'There seems to be enough in there to sustain a Polar expedition.' They'd stopped at a traffic signal, and he was looking in amazement at the amount of stuff she was rummaging about in to locate the phone.

'Phone. Make-up. Sunglasses. Book. Wallet,' Tara said, continuing to rummage. 'Ah, there it is.' She pounced on the phone triumphantly, and looked at the display before answering the call. 'Hi, Lisa,' she said. 'Did you find the gown you wanted?'

Vikram grimaced. Lisa had taken an unaccountable fancy to Tara. On the face of it the two women had nothing in common—Lisa was several years older, far more sophisticated and worldly-wise—but ever since she'd discovered that Tara was an uncommonly good listener she'd gone out of her way to befriend her.

'Yes—I mean, we hadn't got anything planned, really,' Tara was saying. She caught Vikram's eye. 'We were thinking of going out for dinner, and Vikram said I could practise my driving before that...' There was a pause as she listened to what Lisa said. Then, 'No, of course not,' she said. 'I'll ask him and call you back.'

'Lisa wants to know if I can drop by and help her decide on her wedding gown,' she said, turning to Vikram. 'She's meeting her dress designer this afternoon. And can we meet her and Kunal for dinner later on?'

Vikram kept his eyes on the road. Earlier he'd been looking for an excuse to put a little distance between him and Tara—now, perversely, he felt annoyed.

'Why is she asking you for help?' he demanded. 'She hardly knows you. Isn't this something she should be doing with her mother or her best friend or someone?'

'Her mother's in Europe,' Tara said. 'And, I don't know, but it doesn't really look like she has too many friends other than you.' She smiled. 'I guess she doesn't think you're qualified to advise her on wedding gowns. I'm the likeliest substitute.'

Vikram shrugged, not smiling back. 'Go ahead, then,' he said. 'But figure out how to wriggle out of the dinner plan—I'm not keen on spending any more time with her and Wilson than strictly necessary.'

'Because of Vijay?' Tara asked quietly.

Vikram felt a wave of irrational anger surge through him again. 'I don't think we need to go into my reasons,' he replied, his voice rough. 'Now, do you want me to drop you home? Or do you want to be driven directly to Lisa's place?'

'Home,' Tara said. 'I need to do something about the wet clothes I played Holi in.' She stayed silent for a minute more as Vikram swung the car into their lane and pulled up in front of their house. Then her sense of injury at his tone got the better of her. 'Why don't we need to discuss it?' she asked, breathing a little fast. 'You're expecting me to decline a perfectly civil invitation from someone who's your friend, not mine, and you refuse to give me a word of explanation.'

Vikram's expression suggested a man bitten by a butterfly. This was the first time Tara had directly challenged anything he'd said or done, and for a second he didn't know how to react.

'Say that we've already made plans,' he said abruptly.

'That's not the point!' Tara exclaimed. 'I can think up a suitable lie on my own, thanks very much. The point is that Lisa's always on at me about how we should all meet up, and I know you're not keen. I must have made a dozen excuses already. I don't know what the deal with the two of you is—first you tell me she's a close friend of the family, then I find out she was your brother's fiancée, and now you want to avoid her all the time. It just doesn't make sense!'

'Finished?' he asked, his eyebrows raised.

She nodded mutely.

'Let's get a couple of things straight, then. We had a deal, Tara—we talked it over in detail before we decided to marry. I don't think explaining ourselves to each other every step of the way was part of it. I allow you a fair degree of personal space, and I expect the same from you.'

Tara bit back an impulse to tell him exactly what he could do with his personal space. In spite of her frustration with Vikram her heart ached for him. He kept his feelings so carefully shut away from everyone, but the little glimpses she'd got so far suggested that he was hurting badly inside.

'I don't think I'm trying to muscle into your space, Vikram,' she said, putting a gentle hand on his arm. 'I just feel that you need to come to terms with Lisa moving on after Vijay's death and marrying someone else. It'd probably benefit both of you if you spent some time with her and sorted things out.'

Vikram jerked away from Tara's hand as if it was red-hot. 'Stop being so goddamn condescending,' he said, his voice harsh. 'The last thing I need right now is yet another person trying to *understand* me.'

'I'm only trying to help,' Tara said quietly. 'You keep a lot of things bottled up inside you—it might help if you talked about them a little.'

Vikram's eyes were cold, and his tone was deliberately hurtful when he spoke. 'Quite the amateur psychologist,' he drawled. 'Funny how all women come to the same thing in the end—thinking they know what's good for you. I guess I should have seen this coming.'

Tara flinched a little, but her gaze was steady as she met his eyes. 'Right,' she said. 'I get the message.' She opened the car door, and slid out. 'I'll be having dinner with Lisa and Kunal. I guess I'll see you tonight.'

Tara felt her legs tremble as she walked down the drive. Their next-door neighbour was watering plants in her garden and waved cheerily. Tara waved back, trying to smile, as she took out her keys and fumbled at the lock. Once inside, she dropped her handbag and the bag of colour-stained clothes on the floor and sat down on the sofa, taking a deep breath.

'Don't cry,' she told herself fiercely, blinking back the tears that threatened to spring to her eyes.

She sat silently for a long while, going over her conversation with Vikram in her mind. Funny how much words could hurt. She'd always prided herself on her resilience, and had been indulgently contemptuous of the way her mother allowed herself to be cowed by her father. Now it looked as if she'd go the same way herself if she wasn't careful.

The introspection wasn't helping, she thought as she felt her eyes beginning to well up again. Vikram probably cared for her in a superficial way, but somewhere between the honeymoon and now Tara had fallen deeply and completely in love with him. She'd only just fully acknowledged it to herself, and the realisation hurt far more than his words ever could.

Sighing, she picked up her phone to dial Lisa's number. Lisa would have to come and pick her up. Their driver, being North Indian, had taken the day off for Holi, and calling a cab would take ages.

By the time Lisa turned up Tara had regained a lot of her composure. Her heart still ached, and it would have been a relief to unburden herself to someone, but there was no one she could tell. For the first time in her life she felt the kind of loneliness that could come with being in a relationship—talking to even Ritu or her mother about her problems would feel like a betrayal of Vikram.

Lisa's designer had a tiny little boutique in a by-lane in the central part of Bengaluru, and a collection of the most exquisite wedding dresses Tara had ever seen. In spite of her troubles Tara found herself taking an interest. Lisa was still undecided between two dresses, one in a simply-cut classic style and the other a daring, off-the-shoulder affair.

Tara pointed to the first one. 'That's better, I think. The other one will look dated in a few years, and you'll be looking at your wedding pictures for a lot longer than that.'

'That's a good point,' Lisa said, looking impressed. 'All this while I was worried about my older relatives being shocked, but I kept hankering after the more striking dress—now I don't think it's such a good idea after all.'

'You can shock them at the reception,' Tara said. 'That's what I ended up doing, though I didn't plan it that way.'

Lisa laughed. 'I know. Vikram's mum told me the story. She's such a sweetheart. She found it as funny as I did. You're really lucky to have a mother-in-law like her. Kunal's mum is a dragon.'

Tara nodded, not wanting to comment. She liked and respected Vikram's mother, but hadn't spent enough time with her to become a whole-hearted fan like Lisa had.

'Look, she gave me this for the wedding,' Lisa said, digging out a jewellery case from her capacious bag. She clicked the snap open to display a pearl necklace in a beautiful pale gold filigree setting, with tiny diamonds winking between the pearls.

Even to Tara's untrained eyes the necklace screamed out designer jewellery—the setting was unusual, and very well-crafted, and the pearls themselves were large, almost perfectly symmetrical, and a lovely iridescent colour.

'I'm getting the embroidery on the dress done to match the necklace,' Lisa said. 'That's why I brought it along. I badly wanted her to come for the wedding, but she said she won't be able to make it. She did tell me Vikram would come. He will, won't he?'

There was a pleading note in her voice, and Tara thought despairingly *Here we go again.*

'He hasn't told me he won't,' Tara said.

Lisa gave her an unhappy look and turned back to the designer to give her some final instructions on the dress. The wedding was only three weeks away, and there was a great deal of work that needed to be done on it if it was to be ready on time. The designer kept the basic dress styles ready in different sizes, but the bride got to customise the embroidery and the detailing. Privately Tara thought it was a bit of a waste. From five feet away all white-on-white embroidery would look the same, and the dress looked lovely as it was.

'We have time for a cup of coffee before Kunal meets us,' Lisa said as they left the shop.

Tara wondered if telling Lisa she hated coffee would help avoid a *tête-à-tête*. Probably not, she thought, trailing behind Lisa without a word of protest. In any case, it was probably best to allow Lisa to vent about the whole why-is-Vikram-not-happy-with-my-marrying-Kunal thing before she went and said something to Vikram directly.

'He's been avoiding me,' Lisa said. 'I tried calling him a couple of times, but he's always too busy to talk for long. And every time I try to invite him over he says he's travelling or has a meeting or something.'

'He has been very busy,' Tara said

'Even today?' Lisa demanded. 'You said the two of you were planning to go out for dinner, but you're here and he isn't. It's a Saturday, and it's Holi. No one would be working, so you can't say he's got a meeting.'

'Something came up,' Tara replied, hoping her nose wouldn't grow longer by the end of the evening.

'Right,' Lisa said sarcastically, and then leaned across to grab Tara's hand with a remorseful look on her face. 'I'm so sorry, Tara. It must be horrible for you to be caught in the middle like this.'

'Yes, it is,' Tara said baldly. 'Let's talk about something else, if you don't mind. Tell me more about Kunal. I've met him, but I hardly know anything about him.'

Lisa's face blossomed into a smile. 'He's wonderful,' she said. 'I met him at Vikram's house...your house, I mean. But that was before you married Vikram. He'd come over to drop some files off and he offered me a lift home—his flat is quite near mine. Then we ran into each other by accident a couple of times, and he asked me out. I told him about Vijay, and that I didn't date any more, and he was so wonderfully understanding about it all...'

Smart man, Tara felt like saying, but resolutely kept her mouth shut.

'We became really close. I didn't have too many friends at that time, and I thought Vikram deserved a break from me weeping all over him at every opportunity.' Her mouth twisted in a wry smile. 'I told you I handled myself very badly after Vijay died, and Vikram was the only one around to help. I didn't even think of

Kunal as anything more than a friend initially, but we got closer, and when he asked me to marry him I said yes.' Her large golden eyes looked at Tara beseechingly. 'I haven't forgotten Vijay. I never will. It's not like Kunal is a replacement for him. But I was so unhappy, and I do love Kunal—only not the same way—or as much as I loved Vijay.'

'I understand,' Tara said, leaning over the table and patting Lisa's hand. 'And I'm sure Vikram will as well, eventually.' Only she wasn't so sure. Vikram seemed to be completely set against Kunal—it probably made things awkward between the two of them at work, too, an angle which had only just occurred to her.

'There's Kunal,' Lisa said, her face brightening as she looked up.

Tara looked up as well, and smiled at the stocky young man walking into the coffee shop. Lisa and Kunal were a study in contrasts, she thought. Lisa was tall, slim and ethereal-looking. Kunal seemed to have both feet planted firmly on the ground at all points in time. He was also a very shrewd lawyer, going by what she'd heard from Lillian, and he had none of Lisa's rather impractical approach to life. Tara had met him only once earlier, but she'd liked him.

'Happy Holi, people,' Kunal said, kissing Lisa on the top of her head and dropping into the chair next to her. 'Hey, Tara, good to see you again.'

Tara smiled at him. 'Hi, Kunal,' she said. 'Coffee?'

He shook his head. 'None for me—if you guys are done, shall we move to the restaurant? I booked a table for eight-thirty, and Vikram's joining us directly there.'

'I thought he wasn't coming?' Lisa asked, looking from Tara to Kunal.

'I just spoke to him,' Kunal said. 'His meeting was over earlier than planned, so he said he'd be able to make it.'

Lisa's face lit up, and Tara was struck again by how beautiful she was. 'I'm so happy,' she said, turning impulsively to Tara. 'It's been ages since I've seen Vikram.'

Tara didn't say anything, just squeezed Lisa's arm as they got up from the table, hoping her face didn't betray quite how confused she felt. The least Vikram could have done was to have given her a heads-up, she thought, all her carefully suppressed hurt and frustration bubbling over. For a minute she seriously considered dropping out of dinner herself—saying she felt ill or something and going home. But that would only let two other people know that she and Vikram had problems—it wouldn't improve matters between them.

The restaurant Kunal had chosen was inside a large mall, and Tara grimaced inwardly. She found malls a little too soulless herself, and she knew Vikram hated them like poison.

'A herd of buffaloes around a watering hole is more civilised than the crowd in a mall,' he'd told her once, making her giggle. 'It's very difficult to retain any respect for the human race after you see a dozen people clambering over each other to get at the last two pieces of clothing in a discount sale.'

Luckily there were no sales on today, and even the mall was relatively empty for a Saturday evening.

Vikram was already at the restaurant, and he stood up as they came in. Tara heard her phone ping, and she pulled it out to see a message from Vikram—he must have hit the 'send' button the second he saw her.

I'm sorry about this afternoon, Tara read. *I was rude and unreasonable. Forgive me?*

She looked up and met Vikram's eyes. Lisa had already run across the room to hug him exuberantly, and he hugged her back without taking his eyes off Tara. He didn't look repentant in the least, Tara thought, a fresh wave of misery sweeping over her. Whatever had made him change his mind about meeting Lisa and Kunal had nothing to do with her—his apology was probably just to make sure that she didn't create a scene in public. Vikram was shaking hands with Kunal now, and saying something about a recent cricket match. No one would have guessed that a few hours ago he'd been saying he didn't want to spend more than a minute in Kunal's company unless strictly necessary.

'I'll just quickly visit the restroom,' Tara muttered, and scuttled out of the restaurant before she said or did something that betrayed her agitation. Once outside, she located the nearest washroom and darted in, locked herself into an empty stall and buried her face in her hands.

Her phone pinged again.

You OK? the message said.

With trembling fingers, Tara typed back, *Yes. Why are you here? You said you wouldn't come.*

The reply came back a few seconds later. *You were right—I put you in an awkward situation. Trying to set it right.*

You're like one of those all-weather A/C ads on TV. Blow hot, blow cold. Tara typed back.

His admission had made her feel a lot better, but she

was still wary of betraying too much of her own feelings in her answers. She stared at the phone for a minute before it pinged again.

Should I order for you? it said.

Tara felt so absurdly let down she almost burst into tears. She was about to type out a reply when the phone pinged again.

Have a request—can we keep off discussing Vijay or Lisa after this? Only causes trouble between us.

I'll be back in a minute, Tara texted in reply to his first message, and stepped out of the stall.

Her cheeks were burning, and she dipped her hands in cold water from the tap and held them against her face. Nothing had changed. Vikram was just drawing the lines between them a little more clearly—this time he was even documenting what she was allowed to talk about and what she wasn't.

She realised that she was muttering to herself when a teenage girl who'd just entered the washroom gave her an odd look. Tara clamped her lips together immediately and surveyed her face in the mirror. Her face was slightly flushed, and her eyes more glittery than normal, but otherwise she looked OK. She took a tube of lipgloss out of her purse and applied some in the hope that the shimmery colour would draw attention away from her eyes.

Tara plastered her brightest smile on her face as she rejoined the others. Lisa was laughing at something Vikram had just said, and Vikram barely looked at her as she slid onto the sofa next to him—though he put an arm around her and pulled her close. She stayed very still in his embrace, breathing in the scent of his cologne and suppressing an urge to press herself against his warm, hard body. There was no help for it, she thought as she tried to read the menu a waiter had set in front of her. She couldn't prevent herself from being in love with him, and she'd have to figure out a way of dealing with the fact that he had only the most casual feelings for her.

Vikram shot Tara a quick glance. He'd been tortured with regrets after he'd driven off, leaving Tara at the gate of their home. Even while he'd been speaking he'd been conscious of being unfair to her, but he'd been so angry he hadn't been able to control what he said. It had taken him a lot of soul-searching to decide to come and meet Lisa and Kunal. Contrary to what Tara thought, he was there only because he felt he owed it to *her*. And now that he was here it shouldn't be so difficult. All he needed to do was to shut all thoughts of Vijay out of his head and concentrate on the here and now.

He managed to stick to his resolution till halfway through the meal, keeping the conversation as light and impersonal as he could. Then Kunal said something, and Lisa looked up at him with an adoring look on her face so familiar that Vikram's hand clenched around his glass. He had seen the same look in her eyes a hundred times when she was with Vijay, and for a second he hated Lisa so strongly he couldn't keep it from showing on his face. His whole family had rallied around to comfort Lisa after Vijay's death, putting their own grief to the side to help her out of the trough of depression she'd fallen into. She'd seemed devastated then, and now, barely three years later, she'd replaced Vijay in her affections with another man.

Vikram's eyes narrowed, and he was on the brink of saying something unforgivable when he grew conscious of Tara looking up at him anxiously. He glanced down at her and instantly responded to the appealing look in her eyes. He took a deep breath and looked away from Lisa.

'I need another drink,' he said lightly, beckoning to a waiter. 'That Holi party today was quite something.'

Lisa immediately demanded details, and he obliged, telling them about Dr Shanta's foibles in a way that had all of them in splits—even Tara. Tara relaxed slowly. For a second the pure unadulterated hatred in Vikram's eyes had frightened her. Thankfully, Lisa and Kunal had been so engrossed in each other that neither of them had noticed.

Kunal refused a second drink. 'I'm driving,' he said and then, laughing slightly, 'Can't afford a driver like you big-shots.'

'Oh, our driver has the day off,' Vikram said. 'Tara's going to drive us home.'

Tara looked up at him in alarm. 'I don't drive well enough for that!' she said. 'I told you—I can just about change gears and park. And I mess up all the time. My driving instructor gets excited and starts yelling at me in Kannada. I don't understand a word of what he's saying—it's like learning from a Martian!'

Both Kunal and Vikram laughed, though Lisa looked sympathetic.

'Don't worry, you'll be fine,' Kunal said encouragingly.

'Yeah, right,' Tara said, and spent the rest of the meal brooding silently over the ordeal in front of her. Vikram was already a few whiskies down, and though he seemed

perfectly sober he'd fail a breathalyser test—insisting
that he drive was no longer an option.

Tara carefully put the car into gear and edged out of
the parking slot. The mall had parking on the top floor,
and there was a spiral ramp that she needed to negoti-
ate down six floors before she even reached the road.
Strongly tempted to close her eyes, she took the slope
as slowly as she could.

She was negotiating the third circuit of the spiral
when the driver behind her grew impatient and honked
loudly. Startled, Tara swung the wheel a little too far to
the right—and opened her mouth to scream as the wall
rushed up to meet them.

Vikram grabbed the wheel and brought the car back
on track. 'Steady,' he said.

His voice was so gentle and reassuring that Tara
almost burst into tears. 'You're a better driver drunk
than I am sober,' she muttered.

Vikram laughed. 'You'll be fine once you relax a
little,' he said. 'Look—we're on the road now. It won't
be so tough after this.'

Tara nodded, grimly concentrating on the steering
wheel.

'I think a cyclist just overtook you,' Vikram murmured.

Tara took her eyes off the road for a second to give
him a glare. 'There's something wrong with the accel-
erator,' she said indignantly. 'We need to get the car ser-
viced.'

'Maybe if you released the parking brake...'

He was laughing quite openly now, and Tara shot him

a dirty look. 'You could have told me earlier,' she said. 'It's your car that's getting ruined.'

'*Your* car,' he corrected, still looking highly amused. 'And I told you as soon as I noticed.'

He put the radio on and Tara drove the rest of the way in fulminating silence. She heaved a sigh of relief when they reached home and Vikram swung out to open the gate. 'I've a good mind to drive over your toes,' she called out as she reversed into the garage. 'Sadist.'

Unlike most beginners she was good at parking, and she felt positively triumphant as she demonstrated her skills.

Vikram helped her out of the car. 'Knees still wobbly?' he asked, and, when she glared at him, 'Don't worry, driving is like sex. You'll start enjoying it after a while.'

'Who said I enjoyed sex?' Tara said over her shoulder as she marched up the path to the front door.

Vikram was beside her in a second. 'Don't you?' he asked huskily, his hands coming up to span her waist as she unlocked the door. 'You had me fooled,' he said.

He stepped into the house after her, and stayed her hand as she reached out to switch on a light. He bent his head to run his tongue over the seam of her lips, and drew back as she leaned closer to him.

'I guess you don't like this, either,' he said, and nibbled gently at the side of her neck as his hands wreaked havoc on her breasts. 'Or this,' he continued, dipping his head even lower and giving a satisfied growl as her hands came up to fist in his hair and pull him closer to her.

The thought crossed her mind briefly that he was using sex to distract her yet again, but she was past caring as he swung her up into his arms and carried her to bed.

CHAPTER TEN

THREE weeks later, Vikram lounged on their bed watching Tara get ready for Lisa's wedding. She'd elected to wear a simple shift dress in taupe silk, with the diamonds he had given her gleaming at her ears and throat. Her hair flowed in loose waves over her shoulders and she was doing her make-up, frowning into the mirror as she tried to get her lipstick just right.

'You look beautiful,' he said.

Tara looked at him and away quickly. The slight tension between them hadn't abated in the last few weeks. If anything Tara felt things had got worse, with both of them being painfully polite to each other.

'Thanks,' she said. 'Though I think I need make-up classes. I'm smudging this stuff all over my face, and I only just missed spilling eyeliner on my dress. Aren't you getting ready?'

She jumped as Vikram slid lithely off the bed and came to stand next to her, bending down so that his face was level with hers.

'I think you're supposed to do your make-up *before* you put on your clothes,' he said, gently nibbling at the side of her neck.

Tara closed her eyes involuntarily as a little shudder

went through her. 'I'm sure you know all about it,' she managed as his hands went to the zipper of her dress. She gasped as he slid the zipper down slowly 'Vikram, no—we'll be terribly late!'

'We have plenty of time,' he said, sliding her dress off her shoulders very, very slowly. 'Lots and lots of time.' And his lips touched hers, teasingly at first—until she grabbed at his hair and pulled his head down to hers.

Tara's eyes were sparkling when they finally left home, and a careful eye would have spotted that her make-up had been rather hastily done. The church Lisa was getting married in was luckily not very far away, and Vikram and Tara joined the group of family and close friends in the small hall adjoining the church, where Lisa's mum had arranged for a small pre-wedding breakfast.

'Where's Lisa?' Tara asked one of Lisa's cousins in an undertone once Vikram had walked across to speak to some of his office colleagues.

'She's a little upset,' the cousin whispered back. 'You're Tara, right? Can you come with me? Her mother asked me to bring you across as soon as you arrived.'

Tara tensed as the cousin led her across the courtyard to a set of rooms which had been allocated to the bride's family to get ready in. Something was beginning to feel wrong. Two older women who were probably Lisa's aunts were clustered in an outer room, talking in worried undertones, and Mrs Andrews hurried up to meet Tara.

'Come inside,' she said quickly and, taking Tara's arm, led her into a changing room where Lisa was sitting at a dressing table, a make-up girl hovering helplessly at her side.

'I can't do it,' Lisa said as soon as Tara came in. Her whole body was trembling, and her face was whiter than her dress. 'I need to go and tell Kunal I can't marry him. I still love Vijay. This is a big mistake.'

Lisa's mother looked at Tara despairingly. 'That's all she's been saying for the last hour. I've been trying to convince her that it's just pre-wedding jitters, but she refuses to listen.'

It looked far more serious than pre-wedding jitters, Tara thought. Lisa seemed to be on the verge of a seriously scary nervous breakdown.

'Is Vikram here?' Mrs Andrews whispered to Tara, taking her aside for a second.

'Yes,' Tara whispered back, hoping she wouldn't be asked to go and fetch him.

Lisa's mother gave her an imploring look. 'Maybe he could talk to her,' she said. 'He's the only one she listened to after Vijay died.'

Tara took the hint and went out to find Vikram. He was standing with a group of men from the office, obviously talking shop.

'I need to speak to you,' Tara said softly.

He raised an eyebrow. 'Now?'

'Yes, now,' she replied.

Alerted by the sharpness in her tone, he excused himself and stepped into a secluded part of the hall with her.

'It's Lisa,' Tara said without any preamble. 'She says she can't go through with this. She's still in love with Vijay, she says.'

Vikram muttered a curse word under his breath. 'What do you expect *me* to do?' he asked harshly. 'Bring Vijay back from the dead?'

Tara winced. 'If you could speak to her…?' she suggested. 'Please, Vikram.' She put a hand on his arm.

Vikram stood stock-still, looking down at her, an undefinable expression on his face. Tara waited, almost sure that he'd refuse to come with her. Then his eyes flickered a little and he turned away.

'Where is she?' he asked, his voice remote.

Lisa looked up when Tara opened the door. If anything she seemed to be in worse shape than she'd been when Tara had left, and her mother was now sobbing quietly in a corner. Vikram strode to her side.

'You were right,' she said, her voice toneless. 'I've been such a fool—thinking I could move on with life, marry Kunal and be happy.'

'I wasn't right,' Vikram said. 'I've thought about it a lot since we last spoke, Lisa. Vijay wouldn't want you to do this,' he said. 'He loved you and he wanted you to be happy. He wouldn't want you to spend the rest of your life pining away for him.'

Lisa started shaking her head, but Vikram hunkered down in front of her, taking both her hands in his.

'Listen to me,' he said and, as she turned her head away, 'Look at me.'

Tara took Mrs Andrews's arm and gently drew her out of the room. Lisa's aunts and cousins were clustered in the outer room, and she took Mrs Andrews to them before settling down to wait.

The door opened after fifteen minutes and Vikram stepped out. He had a strained look on his face, but Lisa, clinging to his arm, was smiling tremulously.

'Oh, thank God,' Mrs Andrews said, surging to her

feet in a flurry of pink organza, and Tara heaved a silent sigh of relief.

Lisa looked up at Vikram, her eyes brimming over with tears. 'Thank you,' she said, going on tiptoe to kiss him on the cheek.

'You'll need someone to re-do your make-up,' Vikram said, smiling slightly. 'I can't help with *that,* unfortunately.'

'Yes, of course,' Mrs Andrews said, stepping up with tissues and the make-up kit that Lisa had abandoned on the dressing table.

'I don't think we're needed here any longer,' Vikram said, and Tara followed him out into the church grounds. 'Do you mind if we sit here for a bit?' he asked, gesturing towards a bench in a little enclosed patch of garden. 'Or you can go back to the others if you want. I'll join you in a few minutes.'

'I'll stay with you,' Tara said immediately, and then wondered if he wanted her to go. He didn't say anything, however, just collapsed on a bench and threw his head back to look up at the sky. Tara watched him silently. She'd been incredibly moved by the way he'd managed the situation. For all his claims of being callous and unfeeling, when it had come to the point he'd been perfect. God knew what it had cost him to say the words, but he'd made sure that Lisa walked down the aisle to marry Kunal without even the last residue of a feeling that she was betraying Vijay.

A leaf drifted down to land on Vikram's shoulder and Tara gently brushed it off. The gesture made Vikram open his eyes and smile at her. He took her hand in his. Tara sat very still as he shut his eyes again, keeping her hand clasped between his. She felt closer to Vikram at that moment than she ever had to any human being. It was as if her soul had been blundering around in a closed room and someone had finally opened a door and let in the light.

She loved Vikram, she realised. Loved him deeply and unconditionally, just the way he was, with all his flaws and his insecurities and his lack of belief in himself. It didn't even matter if he didn't love her back. Being married to him and being in love with him was enough—it would have to be, at least for now. Vikram might come to love her in time, but right now she couldn't expect more than fondness or physical lust from him.

A mad impulse came over her to lean across and press her lips to his beautiful mouth, and she stayed put only with a lot of difficulty. As if he sensed her emotion, Vikram's eyelids fluttered open. His voice had a dream-like quality about it when he spoke.

'It's like Vijay's finally gone,' he said. 'All this while I've clung on to him, trying to keep him alive in my mind, wondering what I could have done to prevent the accident. Over the last two weeks I've begun to let go.'

'He'd want you to be happy, too,' Tara said, and as he looked at her enquiringly, she flushed. 'Like you said to Lisa that he'd want *her* to be happy. He'd want you to be happy, too.'

Vikram reached out to run his fingers through her hair. 'You're an amazing girl, Tara,' he said softly. 'It must be hell living with someone as moody as I've been since we got married, and I haven't heard you complain once.'

'It hasn't been hell,' she said. 'In some ways I've been

happier with you than I've ever been before.' He looked slightly disbelieving, and suddenly all the pent-up feeling within Tara seemed to burst forth. 'I love you,' she said abruptly.

Vikram's face froze, and Tara felt her heart thud painfully in her chest as she waited for him to say something.

'Right,' he said at last. 'Let's talk once the wedding is over. Lisa should be ready now.'

He got up and held a hand out to Tara. Mechanically she stood up and took his hand, following him into the church. Kunal was waiting at the altar, and the orchestra had just started the wedding march. Tara looked straight ahead of her, nothing really registering in her mind except that she'd told Vikram she loved him, and he'd ignored her. He'd looked shocked, she thought, as if she'd said something distasteful or in bad taste. She shot a glance at his impassive face, wondering what had possessed her.

When Lisa walked down the aisle on her uncle's arm she still looked a little pale, and not quite the radiant bride one would expect. But no one who hadn't seen her earlier in the morning would suspect that anything was wrong. She smiled at them as she passed their pew, and Vikram smiled back encouragingly. Tara felt a fresh pang go through her.

The rest of the wedding went by in a blur. All Tara could remember of it later was that she'd had to try very hard not to break down halfway through the ceremony.

'We can make a quick appearance at the lunch and leave immediately afterwards,' Vikram said in an undertone as the ceremony wound to a finish.

Tara nodded dumbly. She'd been hoping Vikram

hadn't noticed how upset she was—a forlorn hope, given how observant he was.

They were silent in the car, conscious of the driver's presence, and Tara went into the house first. She was sitting in the living room when Vikram came in, her face very still.

'You wanted to talk once we got home,' she said.

'Yes,' Vikram said. 'I don't know whether you meant what you said in the church garden.'

'I did,' she said. 'Though I can see it wasn't something you wanted to hear.'

'Tara, love was never part of the deal, was it?' Vikram said. 'I care about you, but I'm not in love with you.' The stricken look in Tara's eyes pierced his heart, but he forced himself to continue. 'I don't think I'm capable of the kind of love you expect,' he said. 'That was one of the reasons I decided on an arranged marriage, so I could set expectations right from the beginning.'

'I don't have any expectations of you,' Tara said, her voice low. 'I didn't plan to fall in love with you. And I didn't mean to tell you, either—it just slipped out.'

The expression on Vikram's face said that he wished it hadn't, and for the first time since the morning anger began to stir within Tara.

'Well, I'm sorry if my falling in love with you doesn't fit into your blueprint for marriage,' she said sarcastically. 'It's not an experience I'm enjoying, I assure you.'

Vikram stayed grimly silent, goading her into further speech.

'And it'd be more honest to just say you don't love me and leave it at that,' she said, 'instead of feeding me stuff like you not being *capable* of love.'

Vikram's jaw tightened and he said curtly, 'It's the truth. You can choose not to believe me if you want.'

Tara's brows drew closer together, and she'd started to say something when he interrupted.

'I don't think we should discuss this further right now. You're in a bit of a state, and you might end up saying something you'll regret.'

'Saying something that *I'll* regret?' Tara repeated incredulously. 'I think I've already done that, thank you very much. Telling you that I love you was probably the stupidest thing I've done in my entire life.' Her breath coming quickly, she glared at Vikram. 'You're the most cold-blooded person I've ever had the misfortune to meet. I'm not surprised you weren't able to hang on to any of your girlfriends if this is the way you behaved with them.'

'Maybe I didn't *want* to hang on to them,' Vikram said, and his voice was so cold it stopped Tara mid-tirade. 'I'm saying this again, Tara—let's not discuss it until you calm down.'

Tara swung away from him and headed towards the door, wanting desperately to get away from him for a while. 'I agree,' she said, her voice muffled as she swung open the door of the shoe cabinet.

He hadn't wanted to hang on to his girlfriends, she thought, pulling out a pair of flat-soled pumps. Perhaps he meant he didn't want to hang on to her, either.

'I'm going for a walk,' she announced, glad to note that her voice sounded steady and quite calm. Vikram didn't reply, and she opened the front door and went out.

Once outside, Tara walked away from the house as fast as possible. She was perilously close to tears, and had absolutely no idea what she should do next. Going to the institute felt like the natural thing to do, but she knew she wouldn't be able to conceal her distress from the other researchers. And she didn't have any real friends in Bengaluru—just people she'd met socially or through work. For a few seconds she contemplated calling Ritu, then gave up the idea. It wasn't as if Vikram had ill-treated her, or they'd had a fight.

Her heart felt as if it was breaking, and she didn't think she could find the words or the courage to describe what she was going through even to her closest friend. A stray tear escaped and Tara rubbed at her cheeks. Breaking down in the middle of a crowded road wasn't going to help matters, she told herself sternly. Nor could she expect help from anyone else. Being married automatically shut out the rest of the world, even if it didn't bring you any closer to the person you were married to.

An auto-rickshaw honked angrily behind her, and Tara realised that she'd wandered off the pavement and onto the main road. She stepped quickly back onto the pavement and the auto pulled up by her.

'Think you're taking a stroll in a rose garden, do you?' demanded the driver, a large and aggressive-looking man. 'If my auto had touched you, you'd have screamed blue murder—and I'd have been put in jail most likely.'

'No, you wouldn't,' Tara retorted, temporarily nettled out of her misery. 'You'd have made an even bigger fuss than you are now, and I'd probably have had to pay you for breaking my legs.'

'Like the cops would ever take *my* side,' the auto-driver said, pleased to have provoked a reaction. 'A poor man has it rough these days—not like you rich ladies, with your fancy clothes and expensive jewellery.'

'Oh, stop moaning,' Tara said in exasperation. 'Look, are you free? I need to go to Forum Mall.' Her legs were aching, and she was beginning to feel very thirsty. The coffee shop in the mall seemed to be as good a place as any other to regroup and decide what to do next.

'Can't see anyone in the auto, can you?' the driver said. 'Hop in.'

Tara dutifully hopped in and the driver took off, weaving through traffic at an alarming speed. Tara was still holding the clutch purse she'd carried with her to the wedding, and she opened it to check how much money she had. A few hundred-rupee notes, and her debit card. The card was the one linked to the account Vikram had set up for household expenses, and Tara fingered it absently. Vikram had given her everything she could have reasonably expected, she thought. Car, bank account, a lovely home—everything except what she really wanted. She felt numb inside, as if all feeling had deserted her.

'You have enough to pay me, right?' the driver asked suspiciously over his shoulder. 'Once this high-class lady got into my auto, and after I'd driven her some forty kilometres she told me she'd forgotten her purse.'

Tara didn't reply, lost in thought, and he didn't say anything more—though he kept shooting looks at her through the rearview mirror.

'We've arrived,' he said, as they pulled up in front the mall. 'Seventy rupees.'

Tara got out and handed him a hundred-rupee note. 'Keep the change,' she said as he began to fumble in an extremely grimy pocket.

He looked up, surprised—tips didn't come his way

very often. 'Thank you,' he said, and salaamed. 'And, madam…?'

'Yes?' Tara asked.

'Don't look so unhappy,' the man said. 'Everything that happens to us is God's will. Our lives are in His hands.'

Startled by the completely unexpected pious sentiment, Tara stared blankly at him as he restarted the auto and whizzed off, narrowly missing mowing down a careless shopper who'd just stepped off the kerb. Thank heavens she hadn't gone to the institute, she thought, if even an auto-driver who'd never seen her before in his life could tell how upset she was.

His unexpected sympathy had brought her close to tears again, and she blinked them back fiercely. The coffee shop was a bad idea, she realised, unless she wanted to entertain the waiters by salting her coffee with a flood of tears. A movie was a better idea, she thought, scanning the mall directory—at least it would be dark and no one would be looking at her.

Vikram heard his phone ping and picked it up to see a message from his bank thanking him for using his debit card for three hundred and fifty rupees. For a few seconds he thought the bank had made a mistake, before realising that Tara must have used the card he'd given her. The account was in his name, so the transaction alerts came to his phone.

So she wasn't just taking a walk, then, he thought, looking at his watch. She'd been gone for over an hour, and he was beginning to worry. He'd handled the situation badly, and Tara had every right to be upset, but he hadn't expected her to vanish like this. He wondered whether to call her, but then thought he'd give her another half an hour—it was likely she'd be back by then, and he didn't want her to think that he was being overly controlling, calling her up and demanding to know where she was.

Tara shut her eyes and tried to block out the soundtrack of the movie. Ironically, it was one she'd wanted to watch, but now she couldn't bear even to look at the screen. The darkness was a blessing, though. She was in a corner of the movie hall, right at the back where no one could see her, and for the first half hour she'd let the tears roll down her cheeks unchecked. Now she was trying to figure out what to do.

Her first thought had been to leave Vikram and move into the institute hostel, but further thought had shown how impractical that was as a plan. Nothing Vikram had said or done justified her breaking up their marriage. And her parents would be devastated. A daughter who was divorced or even separated from her husband would be a far greater disgrace than a daughter who'd run away from home to study further.

She'd have to go back, however much it hurt her to do so. But not tonight. She didn't feel she could bear it.

By nine-thirty Vikram was pacing up and down the house. It was more than eight hours since Tara had left, and he'd tried calling her several times. The first time the phone had rung but she hadn't picked up. After that he'd been getting recorded messages that first told him the phone was out of coverage area, and then that it was switched off. His phone had pinged a few times—his over-helpful bank, thanking him for withdrawing ten thousand rupees from an ATM and, a little later, for spending six thousand five hundred and thirty-five rupees on his debit card.

He messaged Tara, asking, *Where are you?* hoping she'd see the message and reply when she decided to switch on the phone. The house felt very empty without her, he realised.

His phone rang, and he reached for it eagerly, hoping it was Tara calling him back. It was his mother, however, and his first impulse was not to answer. But it kept ringing and, knowing how she worried about him, he finally picked up.

'Hi, Amma,' he said.

'How was Lisa's wedding?' his mother asked brightly.

Lisa's wedding. He'd almost forgotten about it—it seemed so long ago and so unimportant compared to what had happened next.

'OK, I guess,' he said. At some point Lisa would tell his mother about her breakdown, but he didn't feel like talking about it over the phone.

'I saw some of the pictures her mother loaded onto Facebook,' his mother said. 'Lisa looked lovely. There was one of you and Tara, too. Isn't Tara well? She looked very tired and stressed in the picture. Where is she, by the way? I tried calling her a while back, and her phone seems to be switched off. She hasn't answered any of my messages, either, and that's not like her.'

'She's gone out,' Vikram said through his teeth, cursing Facebook and a world where mothers had access to mobile phones and the internet. If Tara had left him his mother would have to know, but if she was just staying away in a fit of pique there was no reason to get his mum worked up.

'To the lab again?' his mother asked. 'Vikram, I don't have anything against Tara studying as much as she wants, but you need to make sure she doesn't overstrain herself. She works way too hard. You need to take care of her. It's the first time she's been away from her family.'

'Right,' Vikram said, not able to take it any more. 'Amma, I'm sorry, I need to go. I'll talk to you later.'

He put the phone down and buried his face in his hands. He was missing Tara unbearably, and he was worried about her, too. If he was lucky she'd have gone to Dr Shanta, but knowing Tara it was unlikely. She wouldn't want anyone to know how upset she was.

He sat up suddenly. There *was* a way to find out where she was, he thought, picking up the home phone to call his bank.

Ten minutes later he knew that the debit card had first been used at a movie hall in a mall, and that the cash withdrawal had been at an ATM in the same mall. The next time the card had been used it had been at an upmarket hotel on MG Road. His first reaction was relief. She was safe, and if she'd checked into a hotel in Bengaluru she wasn't planning anything drastic like going back to her parents. At least not yet.

His immediate impulse was to follow her to the hotel, but sense prevailed. He didn't know her room number and, while he could quite easily bluff his way past the hotel's guest confidentiality policy, it wouldn't be fair to Tara. She'd left because she wanted to stay away from him, and he should respect that. It was hard, though, and it became even harder when he saw a message on his mobile phone from Tara.

Will be back after a few days. Sorry about this. Need some time to myself. Don't tell parents, please.

He tried calling her, but her phone was switched off again.

Vikram spent a sleepless night, with the day's conversation with Tara spooling relentlessly through his head. He'd been careful to keep his own heart guarded, he realised, but, being a selfish bastard, he hadn't given a thought to Tara's. To be fair he hadn't thought her heart needed guarding. He knew that women found him attractive, and several in the past had claimed to be in love with him. But those were infatuations that had burnt out as quickly as they had flared up, and in Anjali's case she'd ended up hating him. He'd never thought that a woman who knew him as well as Tara did would fall in love with him. He was good in bed, he knew that, but that was all he had going for him.

He went to work the next day, though he was heavy-eyed and had a pounding headache. Something in his face stopped people from asking questions, though, and Justin cancelled a few meetings after taking a long look at him.

'You look like hell,' he said bluntly. 'I don't want you scaring clients away. If you're coming down with something you'd better go home and wait it out.'

'I'm fine,' Vikram said wearily, and went back to his office.

He was dreading going back to an empty house, but he wanted to be there in case Tara came back, so he left work at six. There was no sign of her, and from what he could make out she hadn't come back during the day even to pick up her things. Her cupboards looked undisturbed, and her toothbrush and toothpaste were in their usual place.

The cook had obviously been in the house during the day—yesterday's uneaten dinner had been thrown away and a new one cooked. The table was laid for two, and Vikram's appetite fled as he looked at it. He didn't move the settings, though—there was still a chance Tara might come back later in the evening.

He finally gave up hope around ten o'clock and went into the TV room, mindlessly staring at the screen till exhaustion claimed him and he fell asleep on the couch.

When he awoke it was early morning. The light filtering through the green curtains made the room look like an underwater set from *Titanic*. Vikram sat up and picked up his phone to check his messages. There was nothing from Tara, a couple from work, and yet another message from the bank telling him that his card had been used at the hotel. On impulse he dialled Tara's number. Switched off. He had the hotel number saved on his phone and, feeling pushed beyond endurance, he dialled it.

'Can you put me through to Naintara Sundaram, please,' he said to the operator. 'I don't have her room number.'

Tara picked up on the third ring, sounding groggy. 'Hello?' she said sleepily. 'Who's this?'

Vikram held onto the phone, tongue-tied for the first time in his life. The sound of Tara's voice had unleashed a whole storm of emotions within him—he felt relieved, angry and vulnerable all at the same time. But uppermost was the realisation that he *cared*. He cared about

Tara and he couldn't live without her. Her absence was like a physical ache within him, the agony increasing with every hour she was away. And the worst part was that he didn't know if he'd ever be able to win her back.

The irony of the situation didn't escape him. He'd been incredibly lucky to find a girl like Tara—he'd had the chance to build a new life with her and he'd blown it in every way possible. Even after that she'd fallen in love with him, and he'd blocked her off. He'd been so caught up with his own muddle-headed views on women and love that he'd let the most precious relationship in his life fall apart without making the slightest attempt to salvage it.

'Hello?' Tara said again.

'It's Vikram,' he said, galvanised into speech by the thought that she'd cut the call off if he didn't say anything.

There was a long pause.

'Yes?' she said, and her voice sounded remote and unfriendly.

'Are you OK?'

'Yes.'

Just the single word. No smart-mouthed comeback. His heart thudded uncomfortably in his chest. It might already be too late. If she'd given up on him she'd go and not look back.

'When are you coming home?'

'Home?' Tara repeated, suppressing a hysterical urge to giggle. She'd been wondering if he'd want her back, or if he was so hugely relieved at her leaving that he'd suggest a divorce. It sounded as if he wanted her back, though. 'I told you—I need some time to myself. I'll be back in a day or two.'

He was silent, and for a panicky few seconds Tara thought she'd misunderstood him and he'd been crossing his fingers and hoping she'd say that she wouldn't return.

When he spoke again his voice sounded oddly raspy, as if the words were torn from him. 'I need you back.'

For what? Tara wanted to ask him. Because she was a handy person around the house? Because she nicely filled up the wife-shaped gap in his social life? Because she amused him? She knew she'd start bawling if she got into an argument, though, so she just repeated, 'I'll be back in a few days,' and put the phone down.

Immediately afterwards she took it off the hook and, burying her face in the nearest pillow, surrendered to a furious storm of tears.

Vikram was left staring at a phone that had suddenly gone dead, wondering if he'd made things worse.

Tara got home on Thursday—four days after she'd left home. Her stay in the hotel had helped to the extent that she had been able to think out a course of action. It hadn't helped reduce the pain in her heart, though—it still felt as if she'd been punched in the chest every time she thought about Vikram's reaction when she'd told him she loved him.

It was late evening when she reached home, and she hesitated at the gate for a while. Her courage was beginning to desert her at the thought of having to face Vikram, and she had to stop and take several deep breaths before opening the gate and walking up to the front door. She wasn't carrying a key, and for a few panicky moments she wondered what she'd do if Vikram had gone out, leaving the door locked. But he opened the door a few minutes after she rang the bell, standing aside to let her in.

Tara shot him a quick glance as she stepped through the door. He looked the same, she thought resentfully. He'd probably welcomed the peace and quiet in the house while she'd been away. And, though he wasn't showing it, he had to be gloating about her having come back with her tail between her legs after her dramatic exit a few days earlier. And… She tried to think up some more reasons to fuel her temper, but it was difficult when he was looking at her as if he'd really been worried while she was away. Desperately she tried to hang on to her resentment—it was the only defence she had against him. She was inches away from throwing herself into his arms and bursting into tears.

Probably he realised it as well, as he quietly took her bag from her and moved away. 'Have you had dinner?' he asked.

She hadn't, but she wasn't hungry, so she nodded.

'Do you want to go upstairs and freshen up?' he asked awkwardly. 'I'll clear the dinner things and be with you in a few minutes.'

Tara looked at him a little more closely then, and noticed the dark circles under his eyes, a muscle twitching in his cheek. Not as calm and collected as he looked, she thought, and a mean little part of her was feeling pleased at the thought of his having suffered at least a tiny bit while she was away.

'OK,' she said, and headed towards the stairs.

'Tara?' he said.

She stopped, not turning back.

'I'm glad you're home,' he said.

She didn't reply. Her heart was thudding too loudly in her chest to allow her to speak. He didn't say anything else, and she continued up the stairs without looking back.

She was in bed when Vikram came into the room ten minutes later, and she shut her eyes, feigning sleep. He slid into bed next to her and she felt a warm hand touch her shoulder.

'Tara?' he said.

She didn't reply, keeping her eyes tightly closed.

'Tara?' he said again, sounding weary and a little sad. 'I know you're awake, sweetheart. We need to talk.'

'Not now,' Tara said. 'Please, Vikram.'

He touched her hair lightly. 'I'm sorry if I hurt you,' he said.

Tara flipped over onto her back to look straight into his eyes. 'You can't help the way you feel,' she said. 'But you could give me some space to deal with it.'

'To deal with...?'

'To teach myself to fall out of love with you,' she said flatly. 'I've been thinking about it. Other people fall in and out of love all the time. I'm sure I can manage it. Then we can go back to being the kind of couple we agreed to be, and everyone will be happy.'

Vikram blinked. Whatever he'd expected, it wasn't this. She sounded so matter-of-fact that for a few dreadful seconds he thought that she was already over her feelings for him. Then he noticed her lower lip tremble slightly, and her over-bright eyes, and his heart went out to her.

'I'm sorry,' he repeated.

She sat up. 'Stop saying that again and again,' she said. 'It doesn't help. I told you I'll deal with it. I don't need sympathy.'

Vikram stayed silent.

After a few seconds she said, 'Look, let me move into the spare room for tonight. From tomorrow everything goes back to normal and we pretend the last week didn't happen. Deal?'

'Deal,' he said, wanting to tell her that he was hurting almost as badly as she was, admiring her for the way she was handling the whole mess they were in and, most of all, wanting to take her in his arms and comfort her.

He didn't make a move to touch her, though, knowing that her hold on her composure was tenuous. She'd never forgive him if something he did prompted her to break down in front of him. And it was too early to tell her how he felt. She probably wouldn't believe him anyway. He needed to be sure she was ready to hear it before he plunged into declaring himself.

Tara slid off the bed and gathered up pillows and a blanket. 'Goodnight,' she said, and walked out of the room, leaving Vikram to face yet another a sleepless night.

She'd recently had the spare room done up in cheerful pastel colours, and she looked around it approvingly as she went in. This was all she needed, she told herself. Some time to herself and she'd be fine. As she'd told Vikram, she just needed to pretend that the week hadn't happened.

Having settled this to her satisfaction, she latched the door behind her and, flinging herself onto the bed, burst into uncontrollable sobs.

CHAPTER ELEVEN

TARA woke late the next morning, still feeling tired and heavy-eyed. She'd cried till late into the night, not able to stop even when the tears dried up and her body was racked with dry, hiccupping sobs. Around two in the morning she'd finally fallen asleep, and had got a fitful few hours of rest.

'I probably cried as much last night as I have in the last five years,' she said to herself wryly as she gazed into the mirror.

Her face showed surprisingly little evidence of what she'd been through—her eyelids were slightly swollen, and her eyes weren't as bright as usual, but that was about it. The advantages of youth and being blessed with a good complexion, she thought, splashing some cold water onto her face and brushing her teeth vigorously. Then she inspected herself one last time in the mirror and, satisfied with what she saw, went downstairs with a determined smile on her face.

Vikram was already downstairs. He must have let the cook in earlier that morning as the breakfast table was loaded with a casserole dish full of *idlis,* with a pot of *sambhar* next to it and three little bowls of chutney.

'Good morning,' Tara said airily, sliding into a chair

opposite him and heaping her plate with *idlis*. He looked worse than she did, she thought, giving his rather haggard face a critical look. Anyone would think *he* was the one who'd had a terrible night. 'Has the cook left?' she asked. 'I wanted to tell her to pack lunch for me. I have a full day at the lab.'

'She's left,' Vikram replied. 'She did ask about lunch, but I didn't want to disturb you so I said we'd figure something out.' He'd had an entire night to think about his plan of action, and he'd finally decided to play things by the ear. If Tara wanted to pretend everything was normal, he would, too.

'I'll take some leftover *idlis,* then,' Tara decided. 'She's made enough for a whole troupe of *akhaada* wrestlers.' She looked up and caught Vikram's eye. He had a worried expression on his face, as if he was expecting her to go into meltdown mode at any minute, and she gave him a reassuring and rather saucy wink.

He relaxed almost immediately, his lips curving into a smile. 'Work going well?' he asked.

'Extremely. I think Dr Shanta's almost as impressed at my brilliance as I am myself.' Tara finished her fourth *idli* and got up to find a box to pack her lunch in. 'If I'm lucky I'll be able to move to the next phase of my research before summer is over. I might even be able to get my PhD a little earlier than I'd initially thought.'

She leaned over his shoulder to reach for the chutney and a whiff of his aftershave teased at her nostrils. The familiar scent almost made her lose control. She managed to stay focussed, though, even dropping a light kiss on Vikram's forehead before she moved away from the table.

'I can't wait to be *Dr* Naintara Sundaram,' she said.

'Though I guess people will keep confusing me with a medical doctor and be disappointed when they find out I'm just a botanist.'

'You'll probably do far more good than the average money-grubbing GP,' Vikram said. 'The last time I spoke to Dr Shanta she told me she had very high hopes for you.'

In spite of herself, Tara felt a little glow of pleasure suffuse her face. Damn Vikram, why did he have to start being so unexpectedly *nice* today? As it was, she was finding it difficult not to keep staring at him hungrily all the time. It would have helped if he'd gone into one of his distant moods and ignored her, or replied to whatever she said in monosyllables.

'I'll go and get ready to leave for work, then,' she said. 'See you this evening.'

'See you,' he echoed as he watched her climb the stairs.

He was conscious of a strong sense of loss. Tara seemed like a stranger—a Stepford wife version of the feisty girl he'd married. Perhaps he'd already let things go for too long—he should have followed her and got her back the day she left rather than letting his damn scruples get in the way.

Tara made sure she kept herself busy for the next few days—so busy that she didn't have time to think. She threw herself into her lab work with a vigour that made even Dr Shanta frown and suggest that she not over-strain herself. She gave the house a thorough spring cleaning with the housekeeper's help, and invited some of Vikram's colleagues over for dinner at the weekend, spending the whole day cooking.

Vikram let her do what she wanted, overriding the instinct that prompted him to force things to a head. She was still too vulnerable, he told himself as he watched her rush about in a manic buzz of activity. Mere words wouldn't help—he'd probably end up making things worse. All he could do was try and show her how much he cared for her, and hope that in time he'd be able to convince her of his love.

She was leafing through an old stack of magazines in the TV room when Vikram came home the following Monday. He paused by the doorway and asked, 'What are you hunting for?'

Tara looked up and gave him her most cheerful smile. 'I saw this picture of a bag some weeks back—it looked really cool and I thought I could try and copy it. But I've forgotten which issue it was in, and all the magazines are jumbled up now.'

'Let me try and help,' Vikram said, coming into the room to sit on the other side of the L-shaped sofa. 'Tell me what it looked like.' He didn't miss the look of alarm Tara shot him, but he ignored it—it was about time they stopped tiptoeing around each other and got back to the semblance of a normal relationship. He picked up the first magazine in the heap. 'Crochet bag?' he asked.

'Patchwork, with bits of crochet and bits of cloth and patent leather,' Tara said. 'It was towards the end of the magazine. It's a small picture at the bottom of the page, and the bag's in different shades of beige and brown.'

Vikram started leafing through the pages, putting each magazine aside as he finished with it.

'I'll be travelling next month,' he said after a brief silence. 'First to Mumbai, and then to Madrid and London.'

'OK,' Tara said. 'How long will you be away?'

'Almost two weeks,' Vikram replied, and then said, hesitating a little, 'Now that you've got your passport I was wondering—would you like to come with me? We could take a few days off and go to Scotland. Or we can stay on a bit longer in Madrid.'

Tara gave him a startled look. Vikram had been travelling at least ten days a month since the day they'd got married, but till now he'd never suggested she accompany him. Of course her passport *had* just arrived. Perhaps he thought it made sense for her to come along on an overseas trip.

'I'm not sure,' she said slowly. 'I'm at a fairly critical stage of my project. I don't know if I should be travelling now.'

'Ask Dr Shanta,' he suggested. 'A break might actually be good for you. You've been working really hard of late. Even my mum's being worrying about you.'

'I'll ask,' Tara said, knowing that Dr Shanta would agree with Vikram, but wanting to stave off the discussion.

There was a warm light in Vikram's eyes that was disturbing. If he didn't love her, the least he could do was not look at her like that, she thought resentfully. She watched him from under her eyelashes as he went back to leafing through the magazines. Even looked at objectively he was gorgeous. He was still in his office clothes, though he'd loosened his tie and opened the top button of his shirt. His hair was slightly rumpled, falling carelessly across his forehead, and he looked good enough to eat. Tara imagined getting up and crossing the short distance between them, brushing his hair back and taking his tie off completely, leaning down and pressing teasing kisses to his firm mouth…

'Is this the one?' Vikram asked, his voice cutting across her fantasy just as it was reaching an interesting phase.

Tara jumped slightly and tried to look at the magazine he'd turned towards her.

'Come here,' he said.

She got up and went to him. 'Yes, it is,' she said, not protesting as he pulled her gently down onto his knee.

'You're sure you don't want me to buy it for you?' he asked, nuzzling her neck.

'I like making stuff,' Tara replied, proud that her voice was still steady in spite of the havoc his hands and lips were creating. 'And I value handmade things a lot more than store-bought stuff.'

'Hmm,' he said, turning her a little so that he got better access to the buttons on her dress.

'Vikram…' Tara said, struck by sudden qualms. It was one thing to pretend to be unaffected by him when he was safely across the room, and a completely different thing when she was in his arms. Also, she hadn't made any headway as far as falling out of love with him was concerned, and the feel of his body against hers was driving her crazy. She was at serious risk of losing control and deciding to confess her love all over again.

'You haven't had dinner yet,' she said wildly, snatching at the first excuse she could think of to put some distance between them.

Vikram raised his head and gave her a quizzical look.

'I'm not hungry,' he said, and turned his attention back to the last fastening on her dress. Having disposed of it to his satisfaction, he proceeded to slide the dress off her shoulders.

He lowered his head again, and Tara gave a despairing little groan and surrendered to the tide of sensation that swept over her. The last coherent thought she had was that he only had himself to blame if she wasn't falling out of love with him as fast as he'd wanted.

'Let's take the day off,' Vikram said the next morning.

They were still in bed and Tara stretched languorously, memories of the previous night still lingering in every part of her body.

'The day off?' she repeated. 'You *never* take the day off. I didn't think you knew what a day off was.'

'I do now,' Vikram said, leaning down and kissing her. 'So what do you think? Sound like a plan?'

'What would we do on this day off?' Tara enquired. 'Laze around at home? Go out?'

'Whatever you like.'

He smiled down at her and Tara felt her heart turn over. It was so unfair, she thought. A simple smile from him was enough to set her hormones raging, and it was evident she didn't have nearly the same kind of effect on him. And why did he want to spend time with her now? Wouldn't it make more sense to keep some distance until their marriage fell into the kind of superficially stable pattern he seemed to want?

The questions trembled on the tip of her tongue, but Tara resolutely kept her mouth shut. Blurting out what she was thinking had brought their relationship almost to breaking point once, and the quicker she learnt to curb the impulse the better.

'Well?' Vikram said, trailing a hand gently down her arm. 'Stay in or go out?'

Go out! her brain screamed at her, but she found herself saying, 'Stay in.' She was snatching at every crumb he threw her, she knew that, but the temptation of spending an entire day alone with him was too strong to resist.

'Right,' he said, and slid out of bed.

He was bare-chested, wearing only a pair of shorts, and Tara had a strong impulse to pull him back into bed as she looked up at his superbly muscled torso.

'Put on some clothes,' she muttered, rolling over and pulling a pillow over her head. 'You're a temptation to a good girl, you are.'

He laughed, and leaned across to pull the pillow away. 'Would you like breakfast in bed?' he asked. 'I messaged the cook a little earlier and told her not to come in today.'

'So who's going to cook breakfast?' she asked, tugging the pillow back. 'Or are you suggesting I get up and make it and then get back into bed to eat it?'

'I resent the slur on my cooking skills,' he said as he pulled on a T-shirt. 'Give me ten minutes and I guarantee you'll be surprised.'

She *was* surprised, she thought as she watched him leave the room. Not by the fact that he could cook—he'd lived alone for so many years he'd have to have picked up the basics—but by the way he was behaving. A cosy day at home together was *so* not his thing. If she hadn't known better she'd have thought he was trying to woo her—as it was, she wasn't clear about his motives.

Sighing, she got up to brush her teeth. It was probably

better to take each day as it came rather than trying to over-analyse everything that Vikram did.

Ten minutes later Vikram carried up a tray with a little rack of toast, a bowl of fruit, and a perfectly cooked omelette. There was a glass of freshly squeezed orange juice for Tara, and some coffee for him, and the arrangement of the tray would have been a credit to the room service team of a five-star hotel.

'Nice,' Tara announced as she tasted the omelette. 'Can I assume you'll make lunch as well?'

Vikram shook his head, laughing. 'I'll need some help there. Unless you're OK with boiled vegetables and rice?'

She'd have been OK with eating vegetables burnt to cinders if Vikram was around to eat them with her, but she didn't say so. 'We'll figure something out,' she said, wishing yet again that she didn't love him quite so much.

The morning seemed to fly by. Vikram helped Tara re-arrange the furniture on the ground floor—she'd always wanted to move some of the heavier pieces around, but hadn't been strong enough to shift them without help. With Vikram around all she had to do was point to where she wanted each piece moved and then she was free to stand and ogle at the muscles rippling in his shoulders and arms as he hefted the solid wood furniture around.

'You just asked me to move it *out* from this very spot,' Vikram said suspiciously after a while.

'Yes…' Tara said, not daring to admit that she'd completely lost track of the furniture as she watched him. 'I think it looks better where it was.' He still looked a little suspicious, and Tara glanced quickly at her watch. 'Oooh, look at the time,' she exclaimed. 'I'll start on lunch while you straighten everything up.'

She was halfway out of the door when Vikram caught up with her, moving across the large room as lithely as a panther. He grabbed her to pull her back against him.

'Why do I get the feeling I was conned into doing a bunch of unnecessary stuff there?' he asked, his voice husky against her ear.

Tara leaned against him, shamelessly enjoying the feel of his warm, hard, slightly sweaty body against hers.

'Because you were,' she whispered back. 'I get really turned on watching a man lift heavy stuff.'

After that it was no wonder that all thought of making lunch flew out of their heads—they didn't even make it to the bedroom this time, collapsing in a tangle of limbs on the nearest sofa.

Afterwards Tara lay quietly next to Vikram, her head on his chest so that she could hear the steady thump of his heart. The euphoria of the morning had passed and she was beginning to feel very, very depressed. The more time she spent with Vikram, the more deeply she fell in love with him—and the pain in her heart was rapidly becoming unbearable. She could have dealt with him not returning her love, but the fact that he didn't even want to acknowledge it was what really hurt.

Vikram's breath stirred her hair as he spoke. 'Taking a day off has its advantages,' he said. 'I wonder we didn't think of doing this earlier.'

Tara felt like telling him that he'd been too busy trying to keep away from her earlier, but she held the words back.

'Are you hungry?' she asked instead. 'I think it's almost four o'clock.'

'So it is,' Vikram said, propping himself up to look

at the nearest clock. 'And we've had more than enough exercise to work up an appetite.'

'I'll rustle something up, then,' Tara said, trying to get up.

Vikram pulled her back into his arms. 'Don't bother. We'll order in,' he said. 'Pass me my phone—it's nearer you.'

He pulled her into his arms as he dialled the number of a nearby Chinese restaurant, absently stroking her hair as he placed the order. Somehow the casual caress had the power to upset her more than the most passionate embrace—it suggested a degree of affection that she didn't think Vikram would ever have towards her. Biting her lip, she straightened and picked up the TV remote from a side table. She flicked the TV on, tuning into a completely mindless action flick.

Vikram frowned. 'Do you like that kind of movie?' he asked.

His own tastes in movies ran to the very serious, and she remembered a conversation a long while ago when she'd told him she liked Hollywood romantic comedies.

'There's nothing better on,' she said, shrugging and hoping her voice sounded casual enough.

'Switch it off, then.' He took the remote from her. 'I want to talk to you. I was thinking a little more about my trip next month.'

'The Spain one?' Tara said.

'That's right. I was thinking I could take a couple of weeks off and we could spend some time in Andalusia and then go to Madrid.'

'Sounds interesting,' Tara said, keeping her face averted.

'It would be like a second honeymoon,' Vikram said,

bending down to kiss her lightly. 'Spain's a lovely country. Say yes, Tara. I'll square it with Dr Shanta if you
want. You need a break from microscopes and Petri
dishes.'

'I don't use Petri dishes much,' Tara said, pulling away
from him and standing up. 'Or microscopes, for that matter. I'll speak to Dr Shanta tomorrow.'

She turned towards the stairs and Vikram asked,
'Where are you going?'

'I need a shower,' she called back over her shoulder.
'Anyway, it'll be some time before the food arrives.'

Vikram frowned. Something wasn't quite right, but he
didn't want to push the issue. Tara had suffered enough at
his hands in the past, and now that he was clearer about
his own feelings all he wanted was a chance to make
things up to her.

He flicked the TV on again, tuning into the same action movie that Tara had been watching until the deliv-
ery man from the restaurant rang the bell. He took the
food in and paid the man, tipping him generously before
he closed the door and called out to Tara.

There was no response. The water had stopped running in the bathroom some time ago and he'd not heard
a sound from the first floor since then. Maybe Tara had
fallen asleep—she had good reason to be tired.

He stacked the takeaway cartons on the dining table
and took the stairs two at a time.

'The food's here,' he said, opening the door of their
bedroom, half expecting to see her curled up in bed.

Tara looked up from the suitcase she was packing.
A heap of jeans, dresses and books lay on the bed in an
unorganised pile, evidently having been pulled out from

one of the cupboards in a hurry. A second empty suit-case lay on the bed, next to the one she was cramming clothes into. Vikram stopped at the threshold, completely flabbergasted.

'What are you doing?' he asked slowly, a heavy weight settling in the region of his heart.

'I'm leaving,' she said, closing the suitcase with a very final-sounding thud. 'I'm sorry, I can't take it any more.'

'Take what?' he asked. When she didn't answer he crossed the room in a few quick strides and took her shoulders in his hands, almost shaking her. 'What's hap-pened to you, Tara? I thought we were doing fine.'

He *had* thought that—he'd almost convinced himself that they were over the worst and could look forward to a happy life together. Evidently he'd been deluding himself.

She didn't answer for a few seconds, and then she burst out, her eyes swimming with tears, 'That's the whole point! Today was perfect, only I know you don't mean any of it. You're just trying to make me feel better. I've tried so hard to stop loving you, but it's no use. I'm still just as much in love with you as I was the day of Lisa's wedding. More, if anything. You've no idea how much it hurts. And then you come up with the idea of a second honeymoon—I can't bear it. It's like constant torture.'

The weight lifted from Vikram's heart, and he asked gently, 'Would you still go if you thought I loved you?'

'I'd be all kinds of fool if I thought so, wouldn't I?' Tara said, jerking away from his hands. 'Stop winding me up, Vikram. I've made up my mind, and it'd be more dignified for both of us if you just let me go rather than trying to make me think you care.'

'But I *do* care, damn it!' he said, his voice fierce. As she flinched back, he continued in softer tones, 'I haven't said the words, but I thought you knew.'

'The words are important,' Tara said, not looking at him. 'All this while I thought you were going out of your way to be nice to me because you were just so relieved I wasn't all over you, begging you to love me back.'

Vikram had begun to shake his head even before she'd finished speaking. 'I think I've been in love with you since the night we had that office party. But I was too much of a coward to admit it then, even to myself. All the time I told myself that you weren't really in love with me—it was just a temporary infatuation, and you'd soon realise that I wasn't worth it anyway. But you left instead, and when you came back you told me you were going to teach yourself to fall out of love with me. For a while it felt like we were back to the way we'd been when we'd just got married. I knew by then that I was in love with you. I'd known since the day you stormed out of the house. But I wasn't sure any longer of how you felt. I didn't want to rock the boat—especially after the way I'd handled things earlier.'

'Why would you think you weren't worth it?' Tara asked indignantly, latching onto the one part of his speech that she took objection to. 'Of *course* you're worth it. I wouldn't have fallen in love with you if you weren't, and even if I had I wouldn't have stayed in love with you. You have some really weird ideas in your head about yourself.'

Vikram laughed, bending his head to kiss her tenderly, his lips lingering against hers for a long, long while. Tara clung to him as he finally moved his head away.

'I love you,' he said softly, taking her face between his hands. 'I've been an unspeakable idiot, not telling you the minute I realised it, but I'll spend the rest of my life making it up to you.'

'I love you, too,' Tara said, her eyes filling with tears. She'd been so careful, hiding her feelings from him for so long, and the relief of being able to say the words out loud was overwhelming. 'I love you so much.' The tears spilt over, and she buried her face in Vikram's chest. 'I've loved you since the honeymoon. Only I was so confused—you were so aloof sometimes. I didn't know what to think.'

'I'm sorry,' Vikram said. 'My only excuse is that my feelings for you are so strong it took me a long while to come to terms with them. But I *do* love you, and I know that I'll love you till the day I die.'

Tara nodded, grabbing at a slack part of his T-shirt to scrub the tears off her face. 'I'll have that in writing, please,' she said. 'And you can add in something about being my slave for life. And obeying my every whim and command.'

'Anything you want,' he said.

And as Tara looked into his eyes she saw so much love in them that she forgot about being snippy and put her arms around him.

'All I want is you,' she said softly, reaching up to brush his hair off his forehead. 'For ever.'

'All yours,' he promised, and his lips took hers in a kiss that sent her senses reeling.

Several minutes later Tara pulled away from Vikram and said, 'We should send your dad a thank-you card.' Vikram raised his eyebrows and she grabbed his hands excitedly. 'Don't you see? If it wasn't for that ridiculous ad he put out we'd never even have met!'

'I never thought of that,' Vikram said, much struck by the thought. 'I'll buy him an entire box full of cards as soon as the shops open tomorrow.'

And he did.

* * * * *

ROMANCE

Beholden to the Throne	Carol Marinelli
The Petrelli Heir	Kim Lawrence
Her Little White Lie	Maisey Yates
Her Shameful Secret	Susanna Carr
The Incorrigible Playboy	Emma Darcy
No Longer Forbidden?	Dani Collins
The Enigmatic Greek	Catherine George
The Night That Started It All	Anna Cleary
The Secret Wedding Dress	Ally Blake
Driving Her Crazy	Amy Andrews
The Heir's Proposal	Raye Morgan
The Soldier's Sweetheart	Soraya Lane
The Billionaire's Fair Lady	Barbara Wallace
A Bride for the Maverick Millionaire	Marion Lennox
Take One Arranged Marriage...	Shoma Narayanan
Wild About the Man	Joss Wood
Breaking the Playboy's Rules	Emily Forbes
Hot-Shot Doc Comes to Town	Susan Carlisle

MEDICAL

The Surgeon's Doorstep Baby	Marion Lennox
Dare She Dream of Forever?	Lucy Clark
Craving Her Soldier's Touch	Wendy S. Marcus
Secrets of a Shy Socialite	Wendy S. Marcus

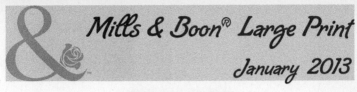

Mills & Boon® Large Print

January 2013

ROMANCE

Unlocking her Innocence	Lynne Graham
Santiago's Command	Kim Lawrence
His Reputation Precedes Him	Carole Mortimer
The Price of Retribution	Sara Craven
The Valtieri Baby	Caroline Anderson
Slow Dance with the Sheriff	Nikki Logan
Bella's Impossible Boss	Michelle Douglas
The Tycoon's Secret Daughter	Susan Meier
Just One Last Night	Helen Brooks
The Greek's Acquisition	Chantelle Shaw
The Husband She Never Knew	Kate Hewitt

HISTORICAL

His Mask of Retribution	Margaret McPhee
How to Disgrace a Lady	Bronwyn Scott
The Captain's Courtesan	Lucy Ashford
Man Behind the Façade	June Francis
The Highlander's Stolen Touch	Terri Brisbin

MEDICAL

Sydney Harbour Hospital: Marco's Temptation	Fiona McArthur
Waking Up With His Runaway Bride	Louisa George
The Legendary Playboy Surgeon	Alison Roberts
Falling for Her Impossible Boss	Alison Roberts
Letting Go With Dr Rodriguez	Fiona Lowe
Dr Tall, Dark...and Dangerous?	Lynne Marshall

Mills & Boon® Hardback

February 2013

ROMANCE

Sold to the Enemy	Sarah Morgan
Uncovering the Silveri Secret	Melanie Milburne
Bartering Her Innocence	Trish Morey
Dealing Her Final Card	Jennie Lucas
In the Heat of the Spotlight	Kate Hewitt
No More Sweet Surrender	Caitlin Crews
Pride After Her Fall	Lucy Ellis
Living the Charade	Michelle Conder
The Downfall of a Good Girl	Kimberly Lang
The One That Got Away	Kelly Hunter
Her Rocky Mountain Protector	Patricia Thayer
The Billionaire's Baby SOS	Susan Meier
Baby out of the Blue	Rebecca Winters
Ballroom to Bride and Groom	Kate Hardy
How To Get Over Your Ex	Nikki Logan
Must Like Kids	Jackie Braun
The Brooding Doc's Redemption	Kate Hardy
The Son that Changed his Life	Jennifer Taylor

MEDICAL

An Inescapable Temptation	Scarlet Wilson
Revealing The Real Dr Robinson	Dianne Drake
The Rebel and Miss Jones	Annie Claydon
Swallowbrook's Wedding of the Year	Abigail Gordon

ROMANCE

Banished to the Harem	Carol Marinelli
Not Just the Greek's Wife	Lucy Monroe
A Delicious Deception	Elizabeth Power
Painted the Other Woman	Julia James
Taming the Brooding Cattleman	Marion Lennox
The Rancher's Unexpected Family	Myrna Mackenzie
Nanny for the Millionaire's Twins	Susan Meier
Truth-Or-Date.com	Nina Harrington
A Game of Vows	Maisey Yates
A Devil in Disguise	Caitlin Crews
Revelations of the Night Before	Lynn Raye Harris

HISTORICAL

Two Wrongs Make a Marriage	Christine Merrill
How to Ruin a Reputation	Bronwyn Scott
When Marrying a Duke...	Helen Dickson
No Occupation for a Lady	Gail Whitiker
Tarnished Rose of the Court	Amanda McCabe

MEDICAL

Sydney Harbour Hospital: Ava's Re-Awakening	Carol Marinelli
How To Mend A Broken Heart	Amy Andrews
Falling for Dr Fearless	Lucy Clark
The Nurse He Shouldn't Notice	Susan Carlisle
Every Boy's Dream Dad	Sue MacKay
Return of the Rebel Surgeon	Connie Cox